The Journey to Nowhere

Unfortunately a true love story of a medico ....

The Journey to Nowhere

Unfortunately a true love story of a medico ....

Diptangshu Das

Srishti
PUBLISHERS & DISTRIBUTORS

Srishti Publishers & Distributors
N-16, C. R. Park
New Delhi 110 019
editorial@srishtipublishers.com

First published by
Srishti Publishers & Distributors in 2010

10 9 8 7 6 5

Typeset in AGaramond 11pt. by Suresh Kumar Sharma at Srishti

Printed and bound in India

I would like to dedicate this book to my love, whose name my heart takes in each and every beat. I love you Sona.....

ACKNOWLEDGEMENT

I would like to say, " *THANK YOU...*" to ,

My parents, Mr. Chittaranjan Das and Mrs. Minati Das, and brother, Arunangsu Das for their great support at all moments.

My friends for being on my side, even in the darkest days of my life. I would like to specially thank, Biswajit Hati (Bisu), for being my first reader, when the whole book was in just the form of a hand written manuscript. Sourav Saha, my best friend, for his kind support and lastly, Arpita Ghatak, for rectifying my mistakes and giving valuable ideas regarding this book.

The editor of Srishti Publishers and the entire team, for giving me an opportunity of a lifetime.

Finally, my acknowledgement would be incomplete, if I do not pay respect to the great musicians and composers, the compositions of whom had been in many pages of the story...

Disclaimer ....

To my utmost concern, I want to say that, this book is not politically motivated. Certain parts of this book might appear to be morally incorrect, but I request all, to simply accept them as a work of pure imagination.

INTRODUCTION

"You are my waking dream....

You are all that's real to me....

You are the magic in the world I see ...."

The phone started to ring .....

"Adi .... Call from your home ....." Prashant shouted....

"What???? At this time? It must be Arun. He is a naughty chap." I said and took the call.

"Hello .... Dad ... wats up? I told you na, I will call you after the meal." I said.

"Hello beta .... Can you hear me clearly?" He asked.

"Ya dad... can hear you clearly. Tell me whats the matter is. You sounds serious." I asked.

"I want you to come home as soon as possible. Nothing serious. Its Pooja who, wants to talk to you. Your mobile was unreachable and she told us to tell you this." He said.

"What are you saying? She should have called me directly, if she wishes to talk to me. Never mind, I will call her after dinner. But I cannot come at this time dad. The practical classes are going on and a single miss takes upon you. The teachers are ferocious. I can't come dad. Let me talk to mom." I said.

"Hi mom... wats up? Tell me, what the actual deal is. Dad seems to be falsifying. It seems that you are trying to hide something from me. Whats that mummy? Tell me." I asked her.

"Please don't laugh. I do not want to talk about anything. I am giving the phone to your dad. Talk to him." The distant voice sounded choked. I could make out easily that something had happened and mom & dad were trying to hide that from me. Mom told me not to laugh, when I was not laughing even at the slightest. I was feeling the heat of the situation. "Hello .... What happened papa? Tell me everything clearly. What happened to her? Tell me. What are you trying to hide from me? Is she alright? Hello ... Hello ....." I shouted.

The silence was broken on the other side. "She had tried to commit suicide. She is fine now. Wants to meet you son. So come fast dear."

"What the hell are you saying? Why did she try to do that? Is she alright? My luck is indeed very bad dad." I said.

"She is well now; I said naaaaa, she wants to talk to you. So come kid. We are waiting for you." Dad said to me.

"Ok... I am coming tomorrow by the first train...." I replied.

INTRODUCTION

"You are my waking dream....

You are all that's real to me....

You are the magic in the world I see ...."

The phone started to ring .....

"Adi .... Call from your home ....." Prashant shouted....

"What???? At this time? It must be Arun. He is a naughty chap." I said and took the call.

"Hello .... Dad ... wats up? I told you na, I will call you after the meal." I said.

"Hello beta .... Can you hear me clearly?" He asked.

"Ya dad... can hear you clearly. Tell me whats the matter is. You sounds serious." I asked.

"I want you to come home as soon as possible. Nothing serious. Its Pooja who, wants to talk to you. Your mobile was unreachable and she told us to tell you this." He said.

"What are you saying? She should have called me directly, if she wishes to talk to me. Never mind, I will call her after dinner. But I cannot come at this time dad. The practical classes are going on and a single miss takes upon you. The teachers are ferocious. I can't come dad. Let me talk to mom." I said.

"Hi mom... wats up? Tell me, what the actual deal is. Dad seems to be falsifying. It seems that you are trying to hide something from me. Whats that mummy? Tell me." I asked her.

"Please don't laugh. I do not want to talk about anything. I am giving the phone to your dad. Talk to him." The distant voice sounded choked. I could make out easily that something had happened and mom & dad were trying to hide that from me. Mom told me not to laugh, when I was not laughing even at the slightest. I was feeling the heat of the situation. "Hello .... What happened papa? Tell me everything clearly. What happened to her? Tell me. What are you trying to hide from me? Is she alright? Hello ... Hello ....." I shouted.

The silence was broken on the other side. "She had tried to commit suicide. She is fine now. Wants to meet you son. So come fast dear."

"What the hell are you saying? Why did she try to do that? Is she alright? My luck is indeed very bad dad." I said.

"She is well now; I said naaaaa, she wants to talk to you. So come kid. We are waiting for you." Dad said to me.

"Ok... I am coming tomorrow by the first train...." I replied.

In the college....

"Hey ... what are you thinking man???" Tanmoy asked suddenly.

I recollected my thoughts and swung in a negative manner.

"What am I hearing dude? She is going to get settled abroad, wants to meet you and you are giving the excuse of attendance. What the bull shit is this yaar? I will manage the attendance. You must go man." He said.

"Yaa.... Bisu was also saying this. But I am in a dilemma, whether to go or not. I don't know whether I could meet her again or not. I am trying to get away man. If I go there, I would be completely lost dude. Actually I don't want to face her." I replied. "I understand your feelings. But can you think what is going on in her mind? She is all alone there. We are always with you to help you, to hold your hand. But she does not have such friends, who could hold her hand? You must go to her. She is going half heartedly and now if you too refuse to be with her she would be completely ruined man...." Tanmoy said.

Before I could say something the ward boy came and informed us about an accident victim going to get admitted in the emergency section. We rushed there at once. The patient was a 14yr girl, who fell from the roof while flying a kite. She was injured seriously. Femur fracture, scapula broken to pieces, ribs fracture but the most potent threat was the skull fracture. The accident had taken place nearly a day before. First they had rushed to district hospital and when the condition worsened, she was brought here.

"Doctor ... will she be alright??? Please tell me doctor. You are our last hope. Please say something." The patient's mother lost control and began to cry. Persons with them tried to console her. I too felt very sorry to hear that, the girl had lost her father 2yrs back.

"We will try our level best. Believe in *God. Uske ghar der hai andher nahin.* We are trying our level best. Rest leave in the hands of destiny. Hope she may fight back." Tanmoy said.

I dragged him back and asked, "Why are you not telling them the truth? Her BP has been down by 20-40, pulse nearly 25-30. She can't survive man."

"shhhh... shhhh ... say quietly. They could have heard it. I know that her condition is beyond our limit. I know she can't make it. But can't we try at our level best? Perhaps she survives." He said at once. "Ok ... I understand that, you wanna try. But ...", before I could say anything more, the nurse came hurriedly and reported that the girl had given up the fight. Her mother was informed. We came outside.

"You fuckers..... Who had made you doctors? Can't save a little girl?" a furious mob encircled us. "Wait .... Wait .... You are making mistakes, we are not doctors yet. The girl had not died of any negligence; her condition was out of control when she had arrived." Tanmoy shouted and tried to restrain the people.

"Don't give false excuses. *Kutte... madar chod ... mar dalon in kamimon ko,"* Shouted someone from the mob. But before they could proceed the hospital super, came with the police and rescued us.

We came out of the emergency building and went straight to the 'rocks', our college's favorite bunking spot. I was completely shocked by the incident. "Chillax man …." Subhro sir said from the back behind. "This is a government hospital. You had to face this many a times." He is two years senior to us. He had been menacing during the ragging season to us. But now he came as a savior. We were both terrified. "What happened to you dude? Take it easy man. Lets drink somewhere in a bar and forget these memories. You are going to be docs. You are certainly going to get into more tougher situations. So *sun yaar chill maar* ." He carried on.

Suddenly Tanmoy started crying. "Heyyyy …wats the matter dude. Don't take it to heart. Even a doc could not do anything in such a situation. You are a student after all. Calm down yaar…." I said immediately. "She reminded me of her. The girl's face resembled to that of Deepa strikingly." he replied.

I remembered that Deepa was his girl friend till last month. She threw him out of her life alleging possessiveness, unsmart nature, rough language etc … etc …

"Are you all ok???", Professor A. Banerjee came looking for us. She is my favorite teacher.. She is the loveliest mam of our college. We have completed the courses from her department, but she remembers each and everyone. "ya … mam … we are all right … nothing happened to us…" We both replied together.

"Ok … relax … go back to the hostel … see you soon." , she said and went away in a hurry. I looked at the time; it was 4:30 pm then. We went away for our hostels.

In the hostel ...

The hostel corridor usually remains empty. But that day there was a large gathering. The students' union election was approaching and both the parties were trying hard to retain their grip in the college. I instantaneously understood that, the worst thing of the today was still to come. But who cares for them, I was deep lost in my memories. I remembered the day when I had last met Pooja in the hospital.

"So .... You came at last." Pooja threw the words, while sitting on the hospital bed.

"What? At last? What is this? You tried to commit suicide. How dare you do this? This is not the first time, you had tried it once before. That can be treated as it had some valid reason. But now you are crossing the limit. You have become completely insane. Didn't you thought of me before taking sleeping pills? What do you think, death is the solution of every problem? What would I do, if something had happened to you?" I asked her in anger.

As was expected she broke into tears. I immediately hold her hands and tried to stop her from crying. But she was in no mood to stop. The next moment, she pulled her hands back and at once hugged me tightly. I too expressed my love to her and was on the verge of crying.

"Ei Sonaaaa ... tell me ... what happened? Why did you take such a rash step?" I asked her. She told that, she had a fight with her parents in the afternoon over her dad's chosen groom Arindam , a CEO in a London based MNC. He was coming to their home to see her; he wanted to get engaged to her. She had refused and her parents beat her up. And then ......

"And ... for this reason you took the path of death!!! Just think about your parents. They are right. You are wasting your life with me. You must leave me. I belong to a middle class family, and yours is a high profile family." I said.

"Stop it.... Leave this matter. Let me have the privilege to give you a very good piece of news. But before that, your Sona wants a kiss." She said. I could clearly make out the glow of happiness in her face. We had been together for quite a long time and I could gauge her feelings. The next moment we were in a lip lock in the hospital cabin as no one, other than us was there.

She started, "Dad wants to talk to you. He had promised that, he will not get me married before I complete my post graduation. He wants me go for studies to Scotland, Glasgow University. This incident had changed his mind probably. He wants to have a talk with you. I didn't know the exact reason. Hey jaanu.. You know, your parents came here in the morning. Dad asked them to visit me. Look at those marigold flowers brought by them. Have you ever told them about my liking to these flowers?"

"Mom dad came here in the morning!!!! They had not told me." I replied.

"Look at yourself. You came here empty handed. What a man are you? Your girl friend is in hospital for you and you don't have they minimum decency to bring flowers or chocolates for your love!!!!! Shame on you ....." she exclaimed.

"Uhhhh .... You make fuss over each and every matter. Ok .... I promise you, the next time when I would come to meet you, I will certainly bring red roses for you." I said. Then I took her in my arms and kissed her.

Suddenly I regained my thoughts and found that a lot of noise was coming from the ground floor. It took me seconds to understand the whole matter. I knew that a conflict was inevitable as both the parties had gathered on the ground floor.

"*Madar chod ..... saala.... Dum hai to samne aa... hijron ki tarah kyun chupa hua hai kutte.*" ...... I recognized the voice. Its of Samir Bhaiyaa. He is the leader of the opposition.

I came downstairs to see what the condition was. My heart sank down after watching the condition in the hostel premises. Many students, belonging to both the parties were injured. Samir Bhaiyaa had got an injury on his forehead. He was bleeding profusely. Ashwini sir, Subhro sir, Nitish sir, Abhijeet sir, everyone was standing by his side. After sometime the police arrived. All helped to take the injured to the hospital. I chose to go upstairs. But the scenes were not going out of my mind. I remembered the words of Dr. A . K . Jalan, our then dean, when the first clash in the hostel took place 6 months ago......

"Shame on all of you... Its shameful to witness such political conflict in a medical college... You are going to be responsible citizens of the society and you are beating each other with sticks. Shame on you boys. Haven't your parents' taught you any manners?

This is a medical college. You are 'would be' doctors. Live upto your reputation. Nowadays each and every person considers doctors to be next to evil due to their behavior and fleecing nature. I thought that you would be different. But you proved me wrong. You want power. Absolute power. What will you do with that? You can't do anything good for society. You proved to be just rotten human beings. You all had ...... leave it ... I do not want to talk to such morons, who can't understand that politicians use them to maintain their vote bank. Poor guys. Hope you understand this as quickly as possible, otherwise if it would be too late, then you would not have anything left."

His words still ring in my ears. Politics in Bengal is very bad. Dr. Jalan was transferred from the college the next week. He was given promotion and sent to a remote hospital as a higher authority. He knew the reason of transfer. Revolt against the customary rules.

"*You are my waking dream....*

You are all that's real to me...." My phone rang and stopped.

I had left my mobile on the bed before going out. I took it and found three messages and five missed calls from Pooja. I opened the inbox to find out that . . . .

The first one went as ....

"*hi ... sweetie... wats up? Wanna talk 2 u.... rply....*"

The second said ....

"*whr r u dear? I wanna talk swthrt... luv u sona...*"

The third one went ....

"*whr r u? ny probs? Why not taking d call? I m getin angry...*"

Immediately I called her.

"*beep ... beep ...beep ...beep ...*"

"Hello Sonaaaaaaa .... Its me....", I said

"Who is me? I don't want to talk to you?" she replied in a heavy voice.

"Hey don't be angry sweetie... at least let me tell the reason why I could not take your call." I said.

"Reason my foot... you must be the thinking of some other girl. I will be out of your life tomorrow and you would be a free bird." She said and again started crying. I always wonder how these girls manage to cry so frequently. I think female lacrimal glands are very sensitive and produce large amount of tears.

"Don't start again.... I was late as a political conflict took place downstairs. So could not take the phone. Sorry sweetheart...." I said.

"Why are you saying sorry? I am sorry Adi. I should have asked you first for the reason you were being unable to take call. Sorry jaanu. Sorry. Sorry. Sorry. Will you not forgive your darling?" she said and as usual I melted. She had mastered this art of making me feel sorry for the wrong she does.

"Ok... Ok .... So what do you wanna say?" I asked.

"I called your mom, she said that you are very upset regarding my departure. She said you don't want to meet me. She told me that you cried to her yesterday. I just wanna say that ...." I stopped her and in a forcible voice said, "Mom told you that I was crying.... Perhaps she had been joking. And regarding your going away, I must say that...... I am happy. A few days ago your parents were determined to get you married straightaway. But now they are letting you go abroad for higher studies. You will be a student of one of the best institutes of the world; your family would be permanently shifting to UK. What can I ask for after all this? I don't exactly know whether I will be able to see you again or not. And the most important thing is that, I don't believe your dad. Pardon me ..... But I don't believe his words. I do not think he will ultimately keep his promise. I think, he is just playing a game with you and me." My voice nearly choked. I tried to hide my emotions.

"Hey you love me so much sweetieeeeee..... Mmmuuu aaahhhhh.... Mmmuuuuaaaahhhhhh. Mmmuuuuaaaahhhhhh.......I love you sona..... Don't be so upset. I know he is playing a game. But this is a sort of success to us dear. I myself, don't believe my dad, how can you? But as I believe in you, I think you must have faith in me. I promise that I will certainly come back to you. And if I find out that there is no going back, I will end my life. I can't belong to any one other than you." She replied.

"How dare you talk like that? End my life!!!! Don't say this again. What will happen to me? What do you think, yours life is only yours? Don't dare to think about such thing again...." I replied instantaneously.

"So you must come tomorrow..." she smiled.

"As you wish my lady... but tomorrow is impossible. I will come on the day you would be leaving. At 12: 00 am midnight. Just as I had wished you on your past birthdays. Remember that the answer of missed call would be switching the night bulb on..." I said and laughed a bit.

"Wow ... that would be great. That's the reason I love you so much. You always do things differently. You are getting very romantic day by day. And don't forget to bring flowers for me. Red roses... Remember??? You promised in the hospital." She said.

"Yaaa... I remember my promise honey. No big deal. I will certainly bring red roses for you. Ok.... Bye ... see you soon..... love you sweetheart...Muuummmaaahhhhh ....Good Bye..." I put the phone down.

Nights in the hostel ....

After her call I was determined to go and meet her. On one side there was the happiness of meeting her and on the other side I was getting engulfed in her memories. I remembered the days we laughed together and the days we cried together. Someone had truly said,

"*Memories play a confusing role in our lives.........*

They make us laugh for the moments we cried together ....

And make us cry for the moments we laughed together..........."

I was completely in a sort of utopia, physically somewhere and mentally elsewhere. Suddenly the door opened with a big sound. Ashwini sir was standing outside with a band of boys.

"Hiiii .... Dude ... are you alright? You came so late. I feared for you. They outnumbered us and beat us up. Otherwise we would have certainly fucked them all. But we succeeded in giving them a very good lesson. They will certainly think first before messing with us. So, how did you get so late???" he asked.

"Nothing sir... there was a fight in the hospital too. But between the patient party and us. The mob took me and Tanmoy as docs and was on the point of beating us. Somehow we escaped as the hospital super arrived with police to rescue us. What about you? What did the police excuse now? I think we must 'gherao' Principal and Dean of Student Affairs and condemn the alleged case of fight in the hostel premises."I replied at once.

"Well said boy... but I am not in any mood of fighting any more. I want to enjoy the victory over them. I want some refreshments. All the drinking party is here. So what do you say... we want a party .... We want a party ...." everyone echoed with Ashwini sir. Ours drinking group comprises of seven seniors and three first yr students, Kunal, Shiva and me.

We had passed many nights like this. No studies, talking bullshit, and drinking with some porn movies running if computer was available. Sometimes we went to prostitutes, only seniors were allowed to have sex, we were barred from it. We were just allowed to see everything from outside the window. Shiva had a lot of interest in that, but to all others' surprise I was happy with my love. I never bothered to go with them. Regarding our drinking habits, I must say that only a gala party could leave us unconscious. Vodka is my favorite. Each had the choice regarding the preferred drink. I always liked to take the first and last shot completely neat. It gave me an electrifying sensation.....

Our party started at 11:30 pm, after the dinner on the hostel terrace.

"Cheers ..... To our success.... Cheers for the courage all of you had shown. Let's fuck them all...." Ashwini sir shouted and at one gulp we all took our first shot of neat vodka.

Vikram sir took out his mobile and started to play a song from the movie JANNAT.

" *Char dinon ka pyar ho rabba .....*

Lambi judai..... tere bin dil mera lage kahin na.... "

The music added to the flavor of the drinks. Kunal had gone completely out of control by then. None of us was so drunk, so early. He always was the first. Whenever we had a drinking party, he gulped down the maximum. I think he always took pride of saying that I have drunk the most and so got knocked out. Suddenly Shiva started shouting.

"You know... loving is bull shit, a foolish act. You meet your love partner and get started. Then gets a heart break and gets separated. A cyclic form."

From the side Subhro sir spoke out, "Well said Shiva.... This love cycle is like the cardiac cycle that is constantly running in our heart. Ya... I am telling this dude as I have experienced a lot. The systole stage signifies the attachment with love and love making phase. Like blood entering the heart someone enters your heart. Then come quarrels and differences, much like the protodiastolic stage. Its like the transient stage or better say intermittent stage. Then comes the diastole stage and everything is gone... Blood is pumped out of your heart to be distributed throughout the body. Your girl leaves you..."

All of us shouted and yelled at such a striking theory relating love and cardiac cycle. Both are related to heart. After we stopped, Shiva started again. He had gone mad.....

"Though a foolish act, we must love a girl of our choice, at least once in our lifetime. Look at this devdas. His paro is leaving him the day after tomorrow.... Oooppsss.... sorry tomorrow... clock had passed 12 naaaa....she is leaving tomorrow... but can anyone see the amount of sorrow and pain in his mind? At least love teaches you a good amount of acting. He had perfected his skills of concealing his feelings. *Kya saahi bola naa?*" he asked me..... " kaminaa saala..... Stop this rubbish. Stop it right now you asshole." I got angry and shouted at him.

Sumit sir realized that the heat was rising. So he stopped both of us and ordered us to go back to the respective rooms. It was 1:30 am then. Kunal was lying down. We knew that, we have to certainly take him to his room. As he is my best friend in college, I always do this duty after the party each time. When I was going to take him up, Vikram sir stopped me.

"Leave him. My room is empty. I will take him to my room. Otherwise you have to carry him to the ground floor." He said. I accepted the proposal at once. Actually his room is on the 5th floor. "Thanks sir. I better go. I have to go home tomorrow. Oh… sorry, today. Thanks for the party. Good night to you all. Bye."

I came down to my room. Avishek was still reading. He was spell bound after watching me completely drunk. He helped me to lie on my bed. I don't remember anything after that.

The extreme shock ....

After such heavy doses at night I slept till 10 am and missed all my classes. My train was at 3:40 in the afternoon. I got up from bed and went to the bathroom. It took me nearly an hour to come back to normal. I had a severe headache. I took two Saridon tablets and went to take my breakfast at 11:00 pm. Our mess manager Amal da was astonished to see me like that. But he soon realized what had happened after I ordered a hot and strong cup of coffee with toasts slightly burnt.

Then I went straight to my room. I wanted to pack as quickly as possible. Everyone from my class had gone to college other than me. I was alone in the room rummaging my belongings, packing what was needed for a two to three day trip. Suddenly I heard a knock on the door. I opened the door and found Kunal standing there. He seemed to be in great pain. He was somewhat in tears.

"Hi man… wats up? Anything wrong? You seems so frenzied." I said.

He stood still in utter silence. I understood something serious had happened. Finally he broke the silence.

"Last night, was I completely out of control?" he asked.

"Ya. You were completely gone. Ooohhhoooooo…. Your dad came naaa? Shit man!!!!" I replied.

"No. He had not. But why did you leave me? Every time you take me with you. But why did you left me at night?" Kunal's voice nearly choked.

"Whats wrong? Vikram sir took you with him. Will you tell me what had happened actually?" I asked him.

"You are my best friend in the college. I can trust only you. Promise me. You will never tell anyone, whatever I tell you." He said. I nodded. He stared at the door, stood up, went to it and bolted it.

"Last night I underwent a homosexual experiences." He started. I put a question mark like facial expression and exclaimed 'what'? He gathered some confidence and said, "Last night at nearly dawn though in a dream like state, I felt that I was completely nude and a hand was caressing each and every inch of my body. It sent shivers all over my mind. As I was completely out of mind I didn't react in any sense. But gradually my sleep broke. It was pitch dark inside the room, only the sky could be seen from the closed window panes. But the pair of hands worked really fine throughout the body. I too got aroused." I stopped him suddenly expressing my disbelief in the story. But tears streamed down his face. There remained no point to think that his story is false.

He resumed. "It was the effect of drinks that had numbed over all my senses. As the hands brushed my genitalia I got completely mad to find, the person who was giving me such a level of satisfaction. I turned and found it was Vikram. He too was completely nude. By then I had been fully aroused. He asked me, if I was enjoying myself. I didn't respond. But he got the positive sign. I was enjoying the whole new experience. He grabbed my dick and started to stroke it. It was a hell down sexperience. I too hold his dick. He directly kissed me on my lips. Our tongues meet. We drank each others saliva. Suddenly he stood up and sat between my thighs. In a blink of an eye I found my cock in his mouth. He was sucking it at the fullest. I moaned and tightened my hips to ensure his full access. I felt a different sensation. It was completely different from the usual masturbation. After five minutes I came in his mouth. Astonishingly he gulped my semen. He came to my mouth and we again kissed. He unloaded my cum in my mouth.

"So from today you are my bitch. Right baby?" Vikram sir said and I responded in affirmative. I then took his cock and sucked it. Nearly 7 inch long cock. I started to play with his balls. After 10 mins he throbbed, and pulled out. Then stroked himself and unloaded on my chest. We slept again embarrassing each other, completely nude."

"What the hell are you talking man? Are you serious? Do you understand what you are saying" I asked Kunal.

"I realize it yaar. So I am telling you all this. It was the effect of wine that had blocked all my senses. I am not gay. I am not homosexual. That's why when I realized all it when I woke up finally nearly at 8, I just ran out of the room." He replied and he put his head down.

"Relax dude. It wasn't your fault." I tried to console him.

"I will kill that son of a bitch. *Mere naase main hone ka usne faida uthaya.* I will ...." He lost his words.

"Chill dude. Chill. You can't blame him. You too enjoyed all the stuff. I admit that he had taken advantage of your unconsciousness, but forget it. After all he is senior. No one is gonna believe you. They will put you in danger. We will keep away from him. But it will be foolish to go against him. Your house is in Mangalore, you can't get out of the hostel. Forget it." I said at once.

"That's why homosexuality should be considered as illegal. They should be hanged till...." He was saying, when I snatched his words and said, "What the bull shit are you talking? Homosexuality is nothing bad. And why should it be? Sexual nature depends on the way the brain acts. There is nothing wrong. I know that my words are definitely hurting you, but you must admit it. Gay marriage is legal in many countries. You have been sexually assaulted by a male, but this does not mean that all gay men are likewise. You can't escape the fact. Even in India voices are been raised for the legalization of homosexual marriage."

"Fuck off. This isn't right. Vikram should not be let off. And you stand for homosex rights???? I thought you have a girl friend naa! How can you say like that? Such persons are nothing but mentally sick. They need medical treatment."

"How can you say that? You are a medical student. You should not talk like that. Homosexual persons are all human and have sound mental condition. You have a wrong outlook. Change yourself. Broaden your horizon of thinking. You may have decision of your own, but similarly it's their right to take decisions. You should understand this." I said in a firm voice. He remained silent and exclaimed a 'sorry'. Later he went away saying just a good bye. I kept sitting on my bed, amidst my clothes and other packing materials, thinking about all the things that had been happening all around me. I felt sorry for Kunal, but there was no way out.

"*Life goes on as it never ends....*"I stood up and left all the thoughts aside to start packing.

The see off by friends ....

All my friends in the hostel gathered in the room. They were nearly 20 in number. All of them knew where I am going. They all gathered to see me off. They came at the expense of their classes. They missed their classes for me.

"So ... you are going finally...." Biswajit said.

"Wish you get your love...." Abhijeet sir yelled and all joined him.

"Thanks to each and everyone, for this see off and of course for always being on my side in every need. Thanks to all man." I shouted. The room broke out with sounds of whistles and clapping.

I remembered the day when I first met these guys. I thought their behavior cheap, but now I like them very much. They also love me, so they made such a nice see off. In the meantime, our seniors had also arrived. Nitish sir shouted, "we all wish you all the best... we will pray that you get her." I got very emotional and hugged Nitish bhaiyaa. I shook hands with each and everyone and was just going to say good bye, when Raj, Suvodip and Arijit came. They had brought a bouquet with them. I was just mesmerized with such a warm gathering of all. I have never done anything for them. But they love me very much. I remembered the days, when they gave my proxy in the open class and helped me in studies. Tears rolled down my eyes, after such a joyous environment. I thanked God, for giving me such good friends. I love them all.

My first date ....

"GANGASAGAR EXPRESS

Departure – 15:40; Platform no. 8"

The time table showed in the electronic board. It was only 2:45 pm then. Still there was nearly half an hour left before the arrival of the train in the platform. I decided to go in the restaurant in Sealdah south. I went there and ordered a cup of strong coffee. I took the first sip and looked at the watch. 2:55 pm, only 10 mins had passed.

The restaurant was completely empty except, me and a college couple of my age at the farthest corner seat. I looked at them. The girl had a very cute smile. On the contrary the boy was looking very much shy. Memories came again in my mind. I and Pooja were a similar sort of couple. She was an extrovert when she was near me, otherwise she was very simple. On the other side, I am extrovert in front of everyone, but when close to her I always get dumbstruck. I remembered my first date. The details are still vivid in my mind.

It was 4th September, 2004 when I was on my first date. We were in class 11, still school kids, going for a date. Before that we had met at many places, school playground, by the side of the dam. But they were not dates...... "Dating —— The contemporary thought goes that, when a boy and a girl go with each other in public and spend quality time with each other, it is called a date." (Definition given by my love guru Subhayan). I was very much thrilled.

After the private tuitions she came to the school playground where I was waiting for her. "Hiiiiiiiiiii ...." I exclaimed. She smiled a bit and came to me. She opened her bag and handed me her English notes copy, the subject that always haunts me. "So .... Congrats again for your success in the national music competition. But I could not understand how they understand your songs? I have heard them in the school annual prize distribution ceremonies, but still I have not understood even a single word....." I teased her and ran away. I knew she would definitely follow me to beat me. "Stop I say or I am going......." She shouted. After this I was left with no other option to stop and watch her playing pranks on me. But she did not do anything as I had expected. She came to me gently and said "Do you remember that we had decided to go no a date today. I don't want to spoil my mood. So can we please go?"

"Hey .... Sorry honey .... I didn't want to hurt you." I nearly begged. She broke the silence with a loud laugh, "I knew that you will come down to me. Actually I only wanted to show you what I am..." she said and laughed again. I understood her prank. In the last 4 months I have seen her playing many types of pranks on me, but today she was innovative. But I always wonder, how she read my mind exactly.... Whatever it is, we started towards the *Sonali Restaurant and Motel,* our site for the date.

On the road we both feared about the suspicious eyes scanning us all around. On the road we walked keeping some distance between us. It went on for few minutes, when she suddenly stopped and said to me, "Hey .... Why are you walking so lazily? Move fast dear. And why are you keeping the distance? Afraid of being caught by someone???"

"No... No... I don't fear anyone. I was just......." Before I could say something she snatched my words saying, "Stop it.... Don't try to fool me. Why don't you say clearly that you are afraid? Mummy's little boy .... Do you wanna lolly pop???"

The man inside me rose and I went to her and without saying anything just held her hands tightly. She tried to free her hand when I spoke, "Wats up? Aren't you happy now?" she was completely shocked by the sudden incident. I could clearly make out her surprise. She failed to hide her expressions; her eyes always spoke the truth. I left her hands and smiled. She made a face to show her agony.

"Now who is afraid?" I asked and started a loud laughter.

"No ... no... nothing... I am not afraid. Whats being afraid off? Its.... It was just a sudden step and I .... I ....just got confused. Publicly you were holding my hands and nothing else." She replied at once.

While we were having such conversations, I noticed many faces turning towards us. Some were laughing and some ignored our presence. I lowered my head and asked her to stop fighting and started to go towards the restaurant. After 10-15 mins we reached our destination. It was nearly evening then. The light had dimmed, the birds were returning to their nests. And here, we the lovebirds were in search of our nest. We took the seat at the corner table away from the door. Actually I was afraid of being seen by someone and have reported at home.

"Two chicken pizza and Two pepsi." She ordered the waiter.

"So.... What did you tell to your parents? I wanna mean, whats the *bahana* today?" I asked her. She laughed and said, "I have told that I am going to Smriti's home for taking the notes."

"Smriti.... Who is that? You have never told me about anyone with such a beautiful name….." I giggled.

"Beautiful name….. My foot…… even I don't know anyone with such name. The name just hastily came to my mind and I just told them that. Thanks God …. There is no one with such name, then you would certainly have left me for her so called beautiful name. You boys are all same. Always go around girls." She said angrily.

"Why are you blaming all the boys? As for Smriti, I was just teasing you. I knew that you get angry quickly. Actually you look horrible when you get angry, like a female ghost." I said and burst into laughter. She also laughed at my silly prank. Suddenly she got serious, hold my hands over the table and said, "Promise me … you will never leave me alone, whatever the conditions be… no one loves me. No one cares for me. My family always wanted a boy, but luck gave them me …a girl. So they do not love me. Keeps me only as an outsider. Only you make me laugh dear. Only you care for me." She said.

"I promise darling. I will never let you alone. I will never leave you alone in any turn of the life. I will do any thing for you dear." I replied and pressed her hand. I saw her eyes getting moist.

"Hey ... you are getting very serious. So you said that you will do anything for me. Then can you bring the moon and stars…. Ohhhhh… sorry …sorry… I just want you to say I LOVE YOU loudly in this restaurant right now in high pitch, so that all can hear that. So can you do that?" She giggled.

"Are you out of mind? Do you think that I have gone completely mad? For your kind information, I am not going to do any such a foolish act." was my prompt reply immediately.

Before she could say anything, the waiter brought the pizza and cold drinks. She put her hand first on the drinks and I on the pizza.

Actually we share a striking difference in the choice of food. We finished and I paid the bill. Astonishingly most of the seats were still empty. So we decided to keep seated there. I ordered ice cream. Vanilla for her and chocolate for me. These cold about things are strictly restricted in my diet as I have serious problem of tonsillitis. But who cares such things when you are on your first date with the girl you love the most. We started talking about our studies, friends, school, family and such usual topics. Casually I looked at the watch and found it was 7:30 pm.

"Hey ....we must return now. If you get late, your parents would tear you into pieces." I said hurriedly. She hurried up and we came outside.

"Wait yaar... we are not still finished. Its customary that, at the end of dating the boy and girl hug each other and say good bye (Subhayan had told me about this). So are you going to hug me or I have to take the initiative." I said and broke into laughter. "What nonsense are you talking? You have gone completely mad..." she said. "Yaa... I am mad for you. Who would not have gone mad with you always hanging around?" I burst into laughter. "Uhhhh..... You are disgusting. I am already late by 10 mins. Hurry up dear." She said and started to walk.

We moved hastily towards her home. I was thinking that, if I had brought the cycle with me, we should not have to walk so fast. I wanted to stop the time. But time... does not stop however you desire. We merely chatted throughout the path. Just exchanged smiles when our eyes met. It seemed that she was thinking something.

Suddenly near the darker alley on the side of the dam, she stopped.

"Why have you stopped now? Walk fast. We are already late. I will take a bus from the school gate and you go home. Are you ok? Your parents often go by this road. If they find you with a boy in these dark streets they will give you the thrashing of lifetime. What are you thinking? Can't you hear me?" I asked.

She said nothing. Stood still for few moments. I was sure that she was thinking of something. Suddenly she came forward, put her arms round me, hugged me and kissed me on my cheek. I was completely taken aback by this sudden incident. As soon as she kissed, she removed her hands and said, "Good Bye…."

"What? I can't get you…." I replied in shock.

She said, "In the restaurant you told that a date is incomplete if the couple does not hug each other, now I had hugged you and our date is complete now. You are such a dumbo dear. Look at your friends and the way they treat their girl friends. They are so romantic. They bring gifts for their girl friends; take them on date by bike. And on the other hand, you, completely different from others. What could I do? Everyone does not have the same kind of luck. It's my bad luck, for which I have got such a jumbo dumbo as my boy friend…. Whatever it be…. Bye ……."

I said 'wait' and tried to hold her hands and hug her. She resisted and quickly moved apart and said, "Stupid … you are a real dumbo. Fool…. Though……. my sweetheart… ok … bye …….."

I stayed still for few moments.

"Excuse me ….. Sir …. Can we sit here?" asked someone and I returned to this world from my thoughts.

"Oh …. Yes …please be seated." I replied and found on the opposite side there was a couple with a cute baby…

The coffee was completely cold by then. I gulped it in one shot and went away. I had a reservation in the train in AC compartment.

I rushed into the train. I took my seat beside the window. There were still nearly 10 mins left for the train to leave. I took out my mobile and put the music on.

"*Tonight we dance.... I leave my life in your hands*

We take the floor nothing is forbidden any more......

Don't let the world dim my sight. .....

Don't let the moment go by, nothing can stop us tonight.....

Bailamos .... Let the rhythm take you over bailamos....."

In the Train ....

My first beer can ....

Suddenly there was an announcement that the train was going to leave 30 minutes later than the scheduled time. Finally it took 15 more minutes to start. The compartment was nearly empty. The seat in front of me was occupied by a man who in his late fifties. He was wearing a nice suit. As soon as the train started I prayed to God for a good journey.

The man was constantly staring at me. I gazed outside. The train was moving very slowly. Three local trains passed the train. After the Bidhan Nagar Road station the train picked up speed.

"Ticket please." The TTE asked hastily. I showed the ticket. He also checked the ticket of that suspicious looking man. On the side berth, a man was sleeping on the upper one. I haven't noticed him before. The man got up and came down. He was completely drunk and was travelling on a monthly ticket. He quarreled with TTE. Police came and took him away.

The man had left but the smell of liquor still lingered as it was an AC compartment. He had certainly taken vodka, my favorite. I smiled at myself and was fast lost in the memories of the day when I had taken vodka for the first time.

It was the winter of class 12. 3rd December. I went for an overnight picnic with my friends. We were 10 boys and 8 girls. She was also in the group. I still clearly remember the moment, when she came to join us. She usually wore salwar suit, but that day she was looking completely devastating. Tight fittings black jeans, creamy white colored top and a black Denim jacket. Her sun glasses were just adding to her beauty. All the boys gaped at her. Sourav smiled at me and patted my back. Actually he is my best friend from the childhood days and only he knew that we were in some sort of serious relation. To everyone else, we were just seeing each other. I went to her and greeted with a gentle smile.

Our picnic spot was calm and cool. As it was a week day, no hustle of any other party wasn't there. We had planned that no cooking would be done. Food was to be brought from the market at the right time. We had packet food material for the dinner.

The tiffin came at 10 am. I put on the music. Pink floyd rocked the party. All boys changed to t-shirt and short pants, as everyone was going to plunge in the river by the side of the spot. The girls remained on the rocks by the side.

We two held hands and stepped in the water. It was very cold, but who cares when your loved one is holding you. Pooja was very much excited about all this, as it was her first overnight picnic. I was happy because it gave us a quality time together. Perhaps she also had this in mind. When I was thinking all these, she pushed me in the water. I got absolutely wet.

"Hey… wats this? You know I have problem of tonsillitis. Why did you plunge me in? Wait …. I will put you in water?" I said and tried to stand up. She again pushed me and ran away on the rocks with the other girls.

I left her and joined the other boys in the pool football… oopss… handball. After sometime, I noticed Asish on the rocks and he was talking to her. He had a serious crush on her and we both knew it clearly. I decided to avoid them, but *dil hai ka manta nahin.* I got annoyed. Still tried to look alright. After few minutes, she rose and went towards the picnic spot. Asish followed her. I was getting out of control. Some of my friends also noticed it. Sourav consoled and asked me to keep patience. But I was losing patience. I waited for nearly ten minutes and then decided to go and look into the matter. A few chattering sounds were coming from behind the bushes.

"What the big deal in it? What does he have, that I don't? Our parents are good friends, our castes match, most of all; we know each other from childhood." I heard the voice of Asish. I decided not to go any further.

"Don't talk rubbish. We are just friends. Its not my problem that you have fallen for me. You are wasting my time and yours. Get off. I can't leave him. I love him." Pooja said politely, still with some annoyance. I was just in the seventh heaven. She is very courageous and straight forward.

Asish remained silent for some time. Suddenly he shouted, "Fuck you." He moved straight towards her and was on the verge of slapping her, when I stopped him. "What is this? You are going to hit her! How can you do that? We are all friends dude." I said.

"Shut up. You mother fucker. I am talking to this bitch. Take your ass away from here." He said angrily. I lost my cool and gave him a tight slap. He at once jumped over me. Others were also there by that time. They stopped us from fighting. I calmed down. But Asish was reluctant. He was just completely out of mind and was talking rubbish.

"Shut up... you bastard." Pooja shouted and slapped him. He calmed down. "You wanted the reason, why I love him so much. You compared yourself with him? Look he stood against you, when you tried to abuse me. You say, you love me. What kind of love it is? You call me 'bitch'!!!! Don't ever try to talk to me." She said and left the place. I followed her.

I ran fast and stood in front of her, made gestures to make her laugh, but she cried. I held her in my arms and hugged her. "Don't be upset sona. Leave it. We are on a picnic and we must enjoy. Hey sonaaaa….. pleaseeeeeeee smile a little for me. Pleaseeeee……." I said. She smiled a bit. We then returned to the spot. Everyone was waiting for us. Asish was too there. He came to us and said sorry. And then he left. I persuaded him, just to give him some moral support. After all we were school friends. We walked past the trees, and suddenly he turned towards me.

"What do you think, I will leave her so easily? Forget about it. I will never let you take away her? If she can't be mine, she would not be yours either. Her parents don't like you naa? What if, I spill the bean in front of them? They will not leave you. Fuck you." He said. I was completely shocked at his behavior. But somehow, I replied "Fuck you too. Do whatever you like. I will face any situation." Both of us left.

"You are looking so serious. What was he saying? Tell me. I will rip him apart." Sourav said in an excited tone. I assured him that, nothing went wrong. But I actually feared the consequences. It was 12 noon by then. We took lunch and went out for sight seeing. We boys selected a place to put the camps for night.

At around 4.30 pm, the sky became cloudy and it started raining heavily. We all took shelter in a temple. To my astonishment, she with her best friend Neha went into the rain and started to dance. Few minutes later, Neha came back. But she was still there.

"Come here Adi..." she called me. I refused. She came back hurriedly and nearly dragged me in the rain. Initially I disliked the idea, but when you are with the loveliest girl, how long can inhibitions remain? I also began to enjoy myself. It was a great feeling. For the first time in life, I was enjoying rain in that fashion. Never before had we danced together. It was simply a great moment.

We returned to the shade. But the harm was done. All the camps had got wet. Seeing us getting wet all our friends had followed. We were seriously in a great problem. No dry dresses. No shelter. But by God's grace, the priest of the temple and his family came to our rescue. They lit fire and helped us to dry our clothes, after the rain stopped. They arranged for our stay in their cattle shed. We did not complain, as it was a great opportunity to all the lovebirds to be together. It was indeed the main funda behind the night out arrangement. Somehow, we all managed. The fire was lit and all sat around it. The cooking department was under Vinit, Subhayan and me. It was fun to see her singing happily. Sometimes she came to me and asked if we required any help. I only laughed as she didn't know anything about cooking. I have learnt some sort of cooking from my scouting days.

We took food at about 9. After that the main party began. Vinit and Subhayan managed to bring nine beer cans and four vodka bottles. I was thrilled as I was going to taste them for the first time.

At once Vinit shouted, "Let me introduce to you all... beer and vodka. All of you have heard about it and some may have tasted it. I request to pick up what you want. Lets enjoy baby...." We all clapped. But I knew the plan of choosing the drink. Actually I was thinking about something. I was confused between beer and vodka. Had never tasted any of them before. Finally I decided to go with beer. I had seen many films, in which the hero gets drunk on vodka. Beer is taken normally. So I went for beer.

"So you took beer? Can I join you?" Pooja asked me. I was astonished to hear something like that from her. I nodded and we walked away to some distance along the side of the river. We walked for nearly ten to fifteen minutes, and in the beautiful clear night the environment itself seemed intoxicating. We sat down on the rocks on the river banks.

As it was winter, the beer can was still cold. I opened the beer can and forwarded to her. She nodded and signaled me to take it first. Hesitatingly I brought it to my mouth and sipped.

"Whack.... Whack.... Its so bitter...." I spitted the drink out.

"Are you alright?" she asked.

"Yaaa... I am OK. Alright. Its taste..... Whack... Very bad. *Faaltu hai.* I better throw it away." I said and before I could respond to what I said, she snatched the beer can from my hands.

"Let me take it." She said and for the first time I noticed hesitation on her face. She trembled for a moment and in a flick of an eye she gulped it. "Cool.... It tastes so rough and strong. I love it." She said and took another sip. I stared at her. I could not believe what I was seeing. I took the can and finally succeeded in taking a sip. It tasted bitter as it earlier had, which was strong and rough to her. I wanted to spit it out, but finally gulped as she was constantly staring at me. But she read the expression on my face and started to laugh. I was completely ashamed and confused. I could not say anything. Again I determined to take it and was going to take it, when she stopped me.

She came close to me and then took a sip from the can. After that I needed no invitation to take it from her mouth. I kissed her in full passion. Our tongues wriggled inside the mouths. It was a completely different sensation. There was no way to spit the beer. I took it in completely and absolutely without any hesitation.

"So... how was the beer from my mouth?" she asked.

I laughed and said, "Formerly it was bitter in taste. But how did you make it so sweet? Your mouth is very sweet. Can you let me take few drinks from your mouth again?" she burst into laughter. I handed over the can to her. She again took a sip from the can and the next moment we again made a lip lock, but this time it lasted for few seconds only. It was dull comparatively than the first one. Then to my astonishment she gulped the whole drink, which was more than half empty by then.

"Now I wanted to taste some vodka." She shouted. It seemed that she had got drunk. But my theory said that she couldn't be drunk already. I exclaimed in astonishment.

"Ya... I want to take vodka from your mouth." She said in ecstasy. After saying that, she rose up and started to walk towards our campfire spot. On the way we stopped and kissed in full passion five times. As we proceeded sounds of laughter and chatter became pronounced. When we reached there, I found a bottle of vodka, waiting for us. None had bothered to take it. She took it and threw it towards me.

"You would require this man." Sourav shouted from behind and threw the cork opener. I opened the cork and took a sip. It felt like alcohol used in homeopathic medicines. If beer was rough and strong, then it was definitely rougher and stronger. We came closer and as the drinks were telling upon us, we kissed each other in full sensation in front of all. I saw jaws drooping down as well as much heartbreak. Sourav just smiled and gave a cheering expression.

That was a great day in my life. I could never forget that day. Even when I take vodka today, I spit the first sip out, then a raw shot.

It was 9 pm then and only half the journey had been completed. I came out of all my thoughts. That suspicious man was still looking at me. I looked and saw someone was rushing fast.

Sudden arrival of Rahul bhaiyaa.....

"Hey ... adi naa ...." , I recollected my thoughts and found rahul bhaiyaa, I had learnt playing cricket from him, he is now an IT professional.

"So, vacations?", he asked .

"No vacations, just wanna meet mom." , I replied.

"So wats up? How is college going on? Is there any probs regarding ragging?and got any gal in life or just on your own? ", he asked.

"whats this bhaiyaa? Can't you think of anything else other than girls? You have not changed even a bit after your marriage. By the way, no girl friend still. College is going superb. Full masti with lots of studies. And ya, before the freshers welcome, the devil of ragging always haunted us." I replied.

"Tell me something about your experiences in the college," he said and sat down beside me. I began with my first day in college. 1st august our classes started. That day our principal gave an introductory lecture and all the HODs took the students to the departments. In the first year we had three subjects, anatomy, the ultimate devil, physiology, the subject one had to fuck up throughout life and at last was biochemistry, nothing special about it.

I was shifted to the maniktala hostel, 20 mins by bus from college. I fell in love at first sight with my room. My room mates were Prashant and Avishek. We mixed up very quickly. But as the night was approaching we were getting nervous thinking of the devil called RAGGING. Suddenly there was a knock on the door. I opened it. There was standing our room senior, Ashwini sir. He is a real blunder.

"Get ready boys, you have to attend the INTRO session in room no.121. So move your ass fast fuckers.", he said and went away with a cigarette in mouth.

"What the fuck is this INTRO?" , Avishek asked.

"Nothing, but an improved version of the so called ragging pratha.... *Chalo gaand marake ate hain* .... We are bound to do it dudes.", Prasu replied.

We went to the room. Before entering I looked at the watch, it was only 6:00 pm then. I was determined to do whatever fuck they would ask me to do, but Avi was very panicky.

"So here come the new students." , someone among the seven seniors in the room, said. "Ok .... Guys ...let's start. Give your complete introduction in shudh Hindi or Bengali. Hmmm ... you start first.", the senior pointed towards Avishek. He made blunder speaking the word 'rank', he got a tight slap. All of us were afraid. I thought of the posters throughout the college, "welcome freshers ....", "ragging is a menace to the society...", and many such, perhaps some of them had been written by these so called 'sirs'. We had been ordered to address them 'sir' till we clear the first year. We have to do whatever they want us to do, without any question. "Go bring cigarettes..." is perhaps their most favorite order. Each day 5 first year students get the duty to do their senior's practical work... Finally they left us at 10:30 for the dinner. Throughout, all we had to do was just to do laugh, pose for some porn movie scenes, remove the clothes and wear them inside out in 2 mins (just like superman, undergarment over pant). During this task I met Biswajit .... A very tough guy. He did not compromise and got out of the room hitting a senior. Later he got a severe thrashing for beating a senior, but he had guts. Next day I made many friends Raj, Subhodip , Esha , Ankita, Dilip , Vivek and lots .....

"woooo .... Nice seniors." Rahul bhaiyaa remarked..

"They are not so bad. Ragging lasted only a week after that we all became good friend. Now every weekend we had beer together and of course wine and vodka. They are very helpful. Always help us in studies. They always kept the first year students away from any political conflict. I know ragging is very bad after a limit. But they never had crossed that limit and I love them all." I said .

"OK ....Now tell me about the girls. I am dying to hear about them." He said.

"In our batch there are only one or two good gals. But I envy our senior batches. Most of the seniors are sex bombs. The canteen is the best place to hang out. It's like a romping zone. These girls can surely melt down any one's pant deep down under....." I replied .

"Ok .... Dude... So ... tell me, had you ever laid off with any gal?" , Rahul bhaiyaa asked at once . I was just taken aback and replied, "No .... I had not done sex yet, but got a chance to see a live telecast when one of our seniors took me with him. As first year students we are not allowed to do anything outside."

"Wow ...... that's great for a little boy? So hadn't you masturbated? Ha .... Ha ..... Ok ... leave the matter. Heard that a political fight had broken out in your college few days ago." he carried on.

"Yaah a fight broke in the hostel premises a week ago and even yesterday. Actually there are two parties, one ruling and the other in opposition ... politics is very bad in Bengal, makes the society rotten. Politics is very bad and deeply entrenched in society in Bengal. It's a rotten part of the society. Remember Prashant, my friend. He had to leave his girl friend due to this politicsbaji ....".

Rahul bhaiyaa asked about the matter enthusiastically. I carried on.

"On the very first day in college, Prasu was clean bowled by a girl named Sananda . They were like made for each other. She was attracted towards him and their story began. They made a humorous couple. He did not understand Bengali and she did not know Hindi. But even I could not understand how they understood each other. I myself started to teach him Bengali. It was always fun to be with them. Tum ki karcho, tumi jabis... all such hind-beng mixture was hilarious. They had a great chemistry between them. Everyone started to talk about them. Actually all were jealous at their bonding. Some of the politician seniors were also fond of her. They played the trick. He belonged to the opposition party, while the women's hostel in which she lived belonged to the ruling party. She was ordered to keep away from him otherwise her belongings would be thrown out of the hostel. But she was not terrified. Prashant also got verbal abuse and some sort of physical torture. But after she was physically tortured, they finally broke up to avoid all this. But still they love each other. The duo still passes hours in class looking and smiling at each other. Prashant didn't compromise with the situation. He was given an option that, if he leave the hostel and became a day scholar, no one would harm him or her. But he didn't leave us. He said, 'Friendship is always superior to me'. I sometimes feel lucky to have such a friend like him.... Here no one thinks for others. Everyone thinks for himself. That's why all the parties are there. Neither the ruling nor the opposition party is good enough to do anything good for the benefit of students, everyone wants power."

"What the fuck is this??? *saale kutte ki aulad, etna gaanda politics karta hain* .... *Oii* ... hear it clearly and always remember, don't get engaged with any girl in college???? But whatever it be, Welcome to this Corporate World....*Bahar se bahut hassen , aur andar se utna hi behuda gaanda... yehi hai asli duniya...* Struggle for existence, survival of the fittest.... *Tere saath bhi kuch hua tha kya*?"

"Truly speaking, yes, I too got engaged in some sort of political rivalry once. But, leave it. Its been nearly six months ago." I replied.

"Whatever it is tell me about it. Let me know how old my brother had become!" he said and smiled gently.

"It was after the first part completion exam, when the incident occurred. After college was over, a friend of mine told me that some seniors were planning to take revenge on me. Actually I had headed a complaint against them for harassing the juniors. But I took it very lightly. But to my surprise, when I was returning from the library, a band of six- seven seniors grabbed my collar, then nearly dragged me to the nearly empty parking lot and then punched me. Before I could react someone again gave a tight slap on my face. By then all my defense systems had started working properly. I hit a senior straight on his nose. It started bleeding instantly. On the next move I punched another. All the others then stopped fighting and at once plunged at me. And restricted all my movements. Their leader then lit a cigarette and blew the smoke on to my face.

"What do you think about yourself? You are the leader! How do you dare to complain against seniors? We can cut you in pieces and throw them in Ganga, no one would ever find you out. If we wish, you could be barred from the college. But, we are not so bad. You only have to kneel down before us and ask for mercy. Go and take away the filed complaint. We will forgive you." Their leader said.

"Uuuhhhhhh. I am scared by your words. Fuck you. What had you seen in Kolkata? College, party office, union and hostel, anything more than that? Nothing? But I have been here for long time. I have been in all the thirteen ghats of Kolkata. You can hit me, break my bones. But you can't kill me. I will recover one day and that day would mark your end. I have enough guts to go to your house and beat you in your room. You are flying high as you are larger in number. But when I would hit you, there will be an equal fight. One upon one. Fuck you all. Do whatever you want. Let me see how much guts you have." I said and in a twisted move hit their leader on the dangerous area of face. He at once collapsed on the spot. Others left me. No one there even showed slightest guts to face me then. All flee away. I took that chap up. By then many of our party members had arrived on the spot. A few of their boys also gathered and then a fight came out as a result. There were nearly twenty of them, but there were just eight of us. But we proved to be heavy weight fighters; all of them were badly beaten. They all had to get medical treatment. On the other hand, only I had to do so. They file a complaint against us. But as there was no evidence about the truth of the incidence. We said that, how could eight students beat twenty students. College authority ordered a high level inquiry committee to find out the truth. Its been recording data regarding the incidence even now. That's it. After that I acquired a rough and tough image in the college. Everyone keeps a distance from me. Everyone thinks twice before talking to me. What would the ruling party think? This question keeps them apart from me. That's all, how I once got in a fight." I stopped.

"Wow. You a have became a man now. Great. Keep up the rough and tough funda. It is said that, if you face everything, you can fuck out everyone in the world. But if you put your arms down, then everyone will fuck you. So … I must say, you had done a great job dude. So, tell me about your friends….." he said.

"Friends. Before coming here, I have only one good friend, Sourav, but here I got lots of good friends. Everyday with them is a fun. I don't know how I could pass my life without them after college…."I answered.

"Lucky guy… you know, these friends are part and parcel of our lives. Without them we can't get on with our life. You are lucky to have such a number of very good friends. I have every material thing, but still I have not been able not to find a good friend. And why are you thinking of the future, just enjoy your college days. Even today, I miss my college days. I always wanted to have a firm of my own, with my friends. But the reality could not let us do that and with the passage of time we got separated. So …." He was going to finish his line when suddenly his phone rang and he rose and said, "Ok … Then man... I have my family in the next compartment, I have to go. Keep in touch. See you soon… *abhi kuch din reh rahe ho to*???"

"No... I am here for only two next days… ok …bye bhaiyaa…"

He went away and I was again left alone to dive into the oceans of memories.

That suspicious man ....

I looked away from the window, at the man in my opposite seat. He was reading a book. The book showed images of the brain, cut at different levels. It was enough to increase my curiosity about that suspicious man. He was looking at me constantly in the initial phase of the journey and was now reading books related to medical background. Suddenly he looked at me and chuckled. I was completely confused by all those behavior of that suspicious person, sitting just opposite to me.

I gathered courage and asked the person, "`Excuse me Sir, may I talk to you?" he nodded and put the book on side. "Sir, from the beginning of the journey, I am finding that, you are looking at me. Do you know me?"

He smiled and said, "Yes son... I know exactly who you are. You study in R.G.KAR MEDICAL COLLEGE." I was shell shocked by that. I don't remember if I had ever crossed this man. "But I am sorry to say that I don't remember you sir. Are you a teacher in my college?"

"Ya. Absolutely right. Do you remember the day when you came in the psychiatry department with Dr. Pratik Chatterjee? I saw you that day during your appointment with Dr. Subhash Dasgupta. I am Dr. L.V.S.R. Rudra Venkataraghavan, HOD of the psychiatry department. So how are you now? You were in serious mental turmoil that day?"

I was completely taken aback by this sudden change of situation. A few minutes ago I was thinking this man to be some sort of rogue, and now he turned out to be a professor of my college.

"Hello sir. I am alright now. The medication helped very much. I am fast recovering from my thoughts. Past… its very much clumsy for me." I replied.

"Ya… I am seeing it in your behavior. Sometimes you look out, the next moment you come back to reality. Sometimes your face turns cheerful and the next moment you get gloomy. You are not completely out of it son. You are still residing in the past. Your eyes tell the truth. Even that day I have noticed the immense amount of pain in your eyes. I have not checked you, but I have consulted Dr. Dasgupta, he says the same thing regarding you. I do not know, what had happened in your past, but try to forget all those. Try to live in present. Your past is painful. But look at the world, there are many people, who are in more pain than you are. Think of your mom and dad, they are living on your hopes. Try to come out son." He said.

I had nothing to say. Just nodded in agreement. Suddenly the train stopped in complete darkness.

"Excuse me Sir, where are you going? This isn't any station. It's the outer only." I asked.

"Actually I am going to the next compartment. The overbridge will perhaps be nearer to that. By the way where are you going? There is no holiday." He said at once.

"I am going home. Some sort of urgent work at home. My home is in Chittaranjan, adjacent to Asansol." I replied.

"Don't fool me kid. Don't lie about the reason of your going. I am a professional psychiatrist. I can sense your lie. Whatever it might be, I just want to say that, come out of your past. Your eyes always look to be in pain. You always think of the past. Your face tries to conceal your pain. But your eyes tell the story. May God bless you kid. Never loose the truth in your eyes and try to forget the pain, the past that haunts you." He said and headed away.

I was completely entangled in my thoughts. I didn't know what to say. Just said, 'thank you'.

The worst day of my life ....

The words of the Professor, kept on buzzing in my ears. That day I was very much depressed due to some sort of family problems and of course the love related problems.

"Uhhhhhhh ...... leave it all...." I said to myself, but completely lost the controls of my thoughts. I dipped in the memories of the worst day of my life. Whatever the conditions were today, things would have been completely different, if things had not gone wrong that day.

"*General Rank – 1440 (All India Engineering Entrance Examination).*"

I looked again and again. I was still not in a state to believe that I had secured such a good rank in the AIEEE exam. I had always wanted to be a software engineer and I was at the verge of fulfilling all my dreams. I was very much happy, as now I was eligible to go to her dad and talk to him with full confidence. I threw a party for all my friends, and everyone was very happy. We two love birds dated each day of the week. But destiny had something else to unfold. And then the bolt from the blue came.

There were five more days for the counselling in the NIT Durgapur. I was determined to take Computer Science Engineering in Nagpur, as my uncle was too from the same college. In the evening I went out as usual to meet her in the park in front of her home beside the dam. I turned to return at nearly 8 pm, when the park closes. There were two roads to my home from the park. One long route through the main road, and the other, a short cut through the darker alleys beside the non resident area. I always take the second one. As I ride my cycle, the short route was my ultimate choice.

I was cycling as fast as I could. Through the darkness I saw a few figures roaming all around on the road. On the side there was a maruti omni and a Tata Sumo. I thought they, might had been going to some wedding party and had halted on the way. Further I was not afraid as I had only my cycle, a 10 rupee note and the best thing was that, the condition of my cycle was such that one would like to return it to me rather than trying it to sell it after repair.

As I was approaching them, I found some sort of suspicious movements. But I didn't stop. The decision for which I regret even today. Like a thunderbolt, something struck me from the back and I fell down on the ground. Before I could react to the situation, someone took me up by my collar and planted a tight fist in my belly. I crumbled.

"What is your name fucker?" the person asked.

"Aditya.. Aditya Verma. Why are you beating me? Look I don't have anything precious in possession. If you want to take the cycle, you can take it. Please leave me. Next week I have counselling for admission in college. Please leave me. I have done nothing wrong. Please leave me. Please….." I replied.

"You have a very precious thing in your possession. Do you know Pooja Malhotra? Ohhhh… hhoooo… Sorry. Sorry. You are her boy friend na? You want to marry her, you asshole…. Now we will show you the cunt. Fuck with it and let the blood dripping down. You mother fucker... don't you realize that, you should leave her, when Mr. Malhotra had warned you? Now we will give you, your much desired punishment, for the wrongs you had done." The person shouted.

I was completely stunned. They were nearly 10 in number, all with sticks, chains, rods in their hands and talking slang. And then came a straight shot directly on my nose. I fell down instantaneously. Blood came down my nose and mouth. I pleaded them to leave me. I told them that I was sorry and would certainly leave her. But they turned a deaf ear towards me. Punches and kicks were coming from all directions like rain. Suddenly, something struck in my hands. It was a chain. I grabbed it tightly and in an instantaneous move I stood up straight. At least three of the goons fell down by the sudden jerk. I punched one, straight into the nose and then struck the one beside him straight into the genital area. "Bang" they were both on ground. I don't know from where all that courage came to me. But, somehow I succeeded to give them a temporary set back. All my clothes were stained by my own blood. There was profuse bleeding from the cuts on my nose, forehead and hand.

"Come son of a bitch. Come one by one. You came so many to fight against one. You fucking assholes. Come one by one and I will show you who the actual mother fucker is. And go and tell your boss, I will fuck him up. Fuck you fuckers." I shouted.

"Look the lion had risen from slumber. You fucking cunt, I will put your head in your asshole." The leader of the goon party shouted. Immediately I began to run. I knew that, if I could cross the bushes and reach the residential areas, I would be back home safely. I ran, but my condition was not such, so that I could run much longer. They caught me and someone hit me hard with a rod directly on my head. I nearly collapsed on the ground. I grabbed someone's leg and bit it. Threw a stone targeting someone. But all was futile. They outnumbered all my efforts to flee. I tried to make a fist and punch one, when a goon strike me on my forearm. After that the pain was immense. I was not even able to move. From all directions I was getting beaten up. Few moments later it seemed that there was no pain and I finally lost all senses.

I opened my eyes for the next time in the hospital, still half awake to all senses. I could barely make out what was happening around. Doctors were moving all around. Mom was crying holding my hand. Screams and cries everywhere.

"Doctor… Doctor… patient no.25 is gaining consciousness. He is blinking." I merely made out the shout of the nurse running out hastily. Till the time doctor came, I had already opened my eyes.

"Where I am? Where are mom and dad? How did I come here?" I put forward all these questions to the doctor, who came in wearing white apron, most probably in his mid fifties. I tried to move, but couldn't due to plasters on my right leg and forearm. A neck collar put my head straight. There were bandages all over on my body.

"You are at Kolkata, B.R.Singh Hospital. Your parents had been informed about you. Don't fear. They could be here any moment." The Doctor replied and gave an injection. It felt nothing. My eyes were roaming all around the room, when I noticed the calendar hanging in the hospital cabin. It showed 3rd august. I couldn't believe the thing I was witnessing.

"Hello sir… whats the date today?" I asked. And the answer was 3rd august indeed. My head just spun around. It seemed that the speed of earth's rotation have gone increased several times. The Doctor understood my confusion and said, "You were in coma for the past three weeks. You are alright now. Don't think of it." I tried to move with double the efforts.

"Relax… relax… you will understand everything gradually. Your parents are coming. Relax son." The doctor said.

"Excuse me Doctor. Let me talk to him first." A police inspector shouted. He was dressed in a clumsy manner, with a physique completely unfit for a police.

"Hello. I am Sudip Mallick, OC, Kolkata Police, investigating your case."

"So… what is your name?" the policeman asked.

"Aditya… Aditya Verma sir." I replied.

"So what happened to you on 13th July? Who had beaten you so much brutally?" he questioned.

I looked towards him with completely blank eyes. Before I could say anything, I had a severe headache and passed out again.

Later on I remembered everything. Mom told that I had suffered four fractures. One humerus (forearm), ankle, frontal bone (skull), and three vertebrae. I had somehow escaped death. I was put on wheel chair, as my lower limbs were completely paralyzed, due to injury in the spinal cord after the vertebrae fracture. Physiotherapy was the only possible treatment. The doctor had said that, there was no certainty whether I could walk again or not. Regarding my narrow escape to death, mom credits my biology teacher, Mr. Sandip Ganguly. That day he was going to a wedding party in his car with his friends. On the way he found the goons beating a guy, which he found to be me. I can only say, it was only the well wishes and prayers of all the persons who love me, that had saved me.

I returned to my home town, Chittaranjan on 17th September,

Vishwakarma Puja day in Bengal. I was on the hospital bed when I saw, Pooja coming into my cabin with a bunch of flowers. She rushed and burst into tears, putting her head on my chest. Mom was standing on my side. She put her hand on her head, as if blessing her. She got up and stopped crying. The next moment I saw my friends coming one by one. Sourav, Vinit, Subhayan, Shankha, Atanu, Nitin, Shree, Esha, Lisa, all were there. My entire school group. All gave a loud applause and rained bouquets over me. I raised my left hand in appreciation. I was very happy to see all my buddies.

"Excuse me.... This isn't a banquet hall. It is a hospital. How did so many of you come to meet a single patient? You are all creating a lot of noise. Please get out. Only two can remain. Please get out of the room." The nurse shouted.

Everyone started to go out, waving good bye. Mom noticed that I wanted her to stay with me. With my hands stretched (on right I was holding her hand from before), I stopped Sourav and her from going away. They are the best buddies of my life. I love Pooja more than my life and likewise I love my best pal Sourav.

"So, how have you passed all these days? Enjoyed naa... none to bore you with silly pranks and age old jokes? I don't think you two ever missed me." I said and smiled. But neither of them was in a mood to play pranks. They were both rather serious. I could see her eyes turning wet.

"No... we didn't miss you, not even once... because you were always with us. We can't lose you dude." His voice trembled.

"Hey man... don't take my words seriously. I was just... leave it. You know my nature yaar." I consoled him.

He resumed, "You wanna know, how I passed my days. I passed

them, crying and lamenting throughout, Because both my best buddies were engaged in a fight against death. They were hanging between life and death."

"What rubbish are you talking man? Two buddies??? Go to nursery class dude. You perhaps had forgotten how to count. I am the first and last of yours buddy raging with death. Who is the other one? Anything wrong?" my voice intensified as the conversation moved forward. I was a bit confused.

"Do you want to know, who was the other one? Then ask her. She can give your answers more correctly. Because she herself is the other one." Sourav exclaimed. "Yes... she tried to commit suicide by cutting her wrist, the day after you were beaten. She rushed to the hospital to see you and aunty just broke over her. She left crying and at home...." He was stopped by Pooja. The next second she again started sobbing. Tears streamed down her eyes to on her lips. She had the most perfect lips I had ever seen. If it had not been a hospital, I would certainly have kissed her. I collected a tear drop from her lips and asked, "Hey sona.... What happened? You tried to end your life, for mom's words? Were you completely out of mind? She was in mental turmoil then. How can you act so foolishly? I love you jaan. How can you do this to me?" I said. "Whatever it be, I am sorry."

In a completely cracked tone she said, "Why are you saying sorry? I must say sorry. I could not understand her feelings. I should not have acted in such a childish manner. I have done all this to you. Look at yourself. You can't even stand on your legs. I am solely responsible for all this. Only me. I tried to kill you. My love tried to kill you." She said and burst into tears.

By then mom had entered the room. She was most probably standing outside the window and had heard everything. She came in and wiped her tears. "I had not told those intentionally dear. I know you two love each other very much, but you will not understand what my condition was, at that time. Perhaps you would not understand till you become parents. If my words had hurt you, please forgive me. I am sorry dear." She said.

" *Excuse me boss.... You have received a text message."*

I regained from my thoughts to see, who had sent a sms.

My college friends ....

I looked at the mobile to find a sms from Biswajit, so called 'Bisu'.

The message goes,

"*hi.... Wats up buddy? When are you reaching? Ani made a complete blunder in the south city mall.*"

I took out the phone and called Bisu. He had set a new caller tune. Some sort of old Bengali song, which I could not understand. Finally after moments of ringing, he took the phone. This relieved me a lot, as I was not wanting to hear that silly oldies song again at that moment.

"Hello... hello... bisu... can you hear me? Bisu ????" I shouted. Some buzzing sound kept floating around. But I could not hear anything from the other end. Finally the connection was lost. I tried to call him, but it said busy. Few minutes later he called.

"Hello... Adi. Wats up dude? Why did you call at this moment?" the distant voice asked.

"Nothing man... Just got your message. And so called. Last time the connection broke suddenly. So whats up with you? What did Ani did now? You said, he made a blunder in the south city mall. Let me guess, girl matter?" I asked.

"Don't talk about that matter. I will surely bang your head on wall. Your so lovely friend, Ani just fucked me up. He is a bullshit fucker. Complete metal head. Leave it." Bisu replied in an arrogant voice.

"Chillax man… tell me what happened? Hello. Hello. Bisu. Can you hear me?" I shouted and meanwhile saw some faces turning towards me. Those faces also include the face of that drunken person, whom police had taken away. He was sitting on the side lower berth. He was not there few minutes ago.

"Hello. Adi. Can you get me? Hello?" Bisu shouted from the other side. "Ya. I get you dude. So, tell me what Ani did in the mall." I said.

"Anirban, your so called Ani, just fucked me up in the south city mall. We two went there just to have some fun after the college. And as usual he got attracted towards girls. There we met two girls, Shina and Shrija. They were damn sexy. According to him, it was love at first sight with Shrija, the younger sister. In this short period time, I have heard his funda of love at first sight at least twenty times. We chatted with them and exchanged phone numbers. I was least bothered about the gals, as you know I am committed to Sneha. But who can make that metal head bustard understand any matter? He had learnt nothing from past experiences in the disco, Park Street. He tracked the girls throughout the mall, in all shops. I decided to wait for him, in the food court. He returned with the gals after an hour. They sat with me and ordered chicken pizza, coke, ice cream, gol gappa bla… bla… bla… and when the time of paying the bill came, he forwarded it to me. Wholly shit, I have to pay a lump some of 550 for his pleasures. Later he says, *dost hi musibaat ke waqt dost ke kam ata hai. bindass raah, bad me de dunga naa…* He got away with the girls and still had not returned. Mobile is switched off. The gals said, their parents were not returning tonight. He is going to have the night of lifetime today." Bisu paused.

"Oh. Shit man. What the fuck are you saying? Sorry to say, but I think you are a complete bull shit, not him. He will enjoy at the expense of your money. I wish, if I had been there with you, I would not certainly let him go alone. He is lucky man. He is going to fuck the beauties today." I said.

"Don't lie to me. I know you dude. You would never have done that. If you had the mentality to enjoy girls, you would have certainly fucked Trisna, the best hottie, sex bomb of our class. Due to your open nature and great academic record, she goes gaga over you. *Hellooo adiii… hi adi. Bye adi… uuuuuuaaaahhhhhh. hahaaaaaaa*" Bisu pranked and laughed.

"Ok… Ok… stop it yaar. I am sorry. Alright. The connection is weak. I will call you later." I shouted. Before he could respond further the connection got lost again. I thought of calling him again, but later on dropped the idea due to some unknown reason.

In the meantime, a sms from Dr. Subhankar Dutta, had came. He is our senior, now a doctor in an NGO. He is still associated with the college party, so visits the hostel often. During such visits our friendship grew. He is a great person indeed, a complete man of principles. In late twenties he is damn smart in outlook. Always wears branded T shirt and jeans, and an ardent fan of classical music, a rare combination.

The sms said,

"hi… its subhankar da. Heard about you in hostel. Hope for the best. Wish you all the best of luck. If possible return before next Monday, because that day we have arranged a medical camp in slums in jadavpur."

I at once repied,

"Thanks... got ur msg. I will certainly rtrn before nxt Monday. Ok. Bye. C u soon."

Medical Service Centre, it is a volunteered NGO run by medical professionals and medical students. I am part of it. This society often arranges free medical check up camps in different parts of the state for the needy and distressed. In times of natural disasters, the members of this society plunge in the rescue work. Subhankar Da brought me to this society. I have participated in such three camps. I was even a part of the relief troop sent to Bihar in the recent flood.

This is my Subhankar da, a man who remains at the beck and call of each and every person. None can imagine what his nature is by looking at him. Many of our seniors say that, he was not like that from the beginning. The story goes that, after completing MBBS, he joined some sort of nursing home in central Kolkata. There he found the original dirty side of the medical profession. He was compelled to prescribe expensive medicines and was ordered to give maximum number of tests in the prescription, even for meager causes. At least patients were rebounded two to three times before their actual treatment began. He could not bear it, and protested against the system. He was thrown out of job on disciplinary charges. But he never stopped protesting. After that he joined a NGO, on a lower salary. He came from a very rich family, and money had never been any problem to him. He now leads a very happy life, has a girl friend with a similar mindset, and most probably plans to marry at the end of this year.

I always admire and respect him. He is a well educated doctor, nice friend and mostly a man of his word. He is my role model in many aspects, but the main thing is that, I do not want to be like him. I do not have such a bold nature. I love him, but I am not a man of principles.

Suddenly the train lurched and stopped amidst complete darkness. The train was running slow from the beginning, stopping at every second or third station. I seldom board this train, but today the train betrayed me. I looked at the watch, it was10 pm. Normally the train reaches Asansol by this time, but today it was late, nearly 1 hour more would require to reach Asansol, if the train moves at full pace. But the destiny might have something more to unfold that night and the train has now been completely stopped.

Few phone calls ....

I stood up and went to the toilet. Most of the seats were empty. I saw that the drunken person was still fast asleep. I too was feeling very tired. I lay on my seat. But how could sleep come, at such moments? I was losing patience, and was thinking only, when the train would start again. Nearly half an hour passed. I kept lying and prayed to the Almighty, to recover the damage as soon as possible, and let me reach my destination. After a few minutes, a tea vendor came. I took tea and some snacks. He said that, due to some engine damage the train had stopped. It would certainly take another hour to repair it. I was very hungry as I had already taken my dinner at 9, when the railway men served it. I took out some biscuits and started to nibble them. But my mind was elsewhere.

I took the phone out and called papa.

"Hello... papa. There has been an engine breakdown near Durgapur and I am going to be indefinitely late." I said.

"What? Engine breakdown, near Durgapur? Ok. When are you expecting the train to come here?" he asked.

"Can't say. Its been nearly an hour that the mechanics are trying to repair it. Its still a two hour journey, from here to home. I think by 1am I would reach home. Please come to station with food, my blue T shirt and my new cycle. I will directly go to meet her from the station. Ok? Did you get it???" I asked. But no one answered. "Hello... dad... can you hear me?"

"Ok son. I will be there on time. But.... Are you sure, you want to go there at night. You know Pooja's parents very well. If they get slightest hint of your meeting, they will rip you two apart. They are very dangerous kid." Dad said in an utter confused state of mind.

"Don't think so much dad. I will be alright. I will manage everything. We have planned well. And for your kind information, I went to meet her many times at night in class 12, you don't even have any trace of it. You are completely unaware naaa......" I said and laughed.

"What the hell are you talking about? You went to meet her at night and I thought you were staying in your room. Come home, if they spare you, I will kill you. Where from do you got so much courage? I will tell your mummy." He said in an arrogant mood, still in a light way.

"Sorry dad, I have inherited this courage from you. Mom had told me that you went to meet her in the night before the marriage. I am your worthy son. Am I wrong dad?" I broke into laughter.

"Your mom naaa.. She is teaching all this bull shit to you. I will definitely...", before he could say anything more, I said, "Sorry dad. I know you are hurt. But I can't live without her. I have to go. Please. Don't mind. I will return safe dad." My voice nearly crumpled.

"Hey son... don't take it so seriously. I was just joking. And for your kind information, I knew everything. Mom had told me. I always had faith in you and that's why I have never forbidden you from going there. You are actually my worthy son. Be a brave man like your dad. Inspite of being from a different caste, I married a

Bihari girl 20 yrs back against the wish of everyone. At that time love was a sin. If I could succeed, you will attain success my child. My blessings are always with you." His voice lowered. I understood that, he might have been feeling bad by then.

"Ok. Enough show off dad. Leave the matter. You positively come on time. And call the driver and check the car. Because, your car is the eighth wonder of the world. It gets damaged whenever it is required the most." I said and chuckled a bit.

"Don't say anything about my car. I have told you many times. I asked you to get a bike, but you refused. Don't blame me. I have taken you to nursery school in that car. You have taken your board exams after traveling to the centre on that car." he said.

"Ohhooooo... I think your memory has become like a sieve. Don't you remember, that the car broke down mid way, while going to the centre for WBJEE exam and we had to take a lift from a passing car?" I pranked on dad.

"You can't judge it by a single incident. It still gives mileage of nearly 10, after 20 yrs of service." He said.

"Ok. Sorry. I should have thought before talking anything to you about your 'wonderful' car. Forget the matter. Be at the station in time. And the last thing, don't bring mom with you. It's my request dad. Please, manage mom. She will never let me go. Pleaseeeeeeeee." I humbly requested.

"Ya I will manage the matter. But promise me, you will never say anything wrong about my car. If you agree, I will come." he said. I did not negotiate any further talks and accepted his proposal at once.

I disconnected the phone and dialed the number 09874451264. Its her number. The phone rang, but no one picked it up. I again called, and the same result. The train gave a jerk suddenly. I realized that, the train would resume its journey at any moment. I waited for nearly five minutes and called her again.

"Hello.... Hello.... Poo can you hear me? Hello......" I said, before any reply could come the connection failed again. I tried to call her again. Once I thought of not calling her, but instantly I remembered that she would be gone the next day. Then we might not be able to talk again in the future. My heart sank completely with the thought of losing her. It seemed as if some deep cut had been opened up, causing immense pain, a deep burning sensation.

In the meantime the train started. It was 11.15 pm by my watch. Unconsciously a few tears came down my face. I wiped them to avoid any unwanted attention from a co passenger. I tried to call her again, but this time it said that, the phone is busy. I thought she might have been calling me. But her call did not come.

" *Excuse me boss .... you have received a text message.*"

I hurriedly opened the message. It was actually from her.

"*hi... got u out of network. So called ur mom. U hv nt said her dat u r coming 2 met me??? Its bad. U sud hv tell her. I luv u jaanu. U know, D son of bitch hv came. He will go with us 2 delhi. I will kill him. Luv u sweetie... mmmuuuaaaahhhhhhh.*"

I realized the whole matter. Her father's much desired CEO groom had came to see them off, or better say butter her out. Before I could reply she sent another message.

"*u r coming naa... plz cum. I want 2 pass d nite wid u. plz cum. Its d last time of my life when I will b laughing. Plz cum dear. Plz mmmuuuuaaahhhhh. mmuuaaaaaahhhhhhh.*"

I got the whole matter. She talked to mom, and mom messed the whole situation. But mom can't be blamed. She fears for me, mostly after all the incidents of the past she does not believe her parent's words. I answered her,

"I m coming sweetie. Wait 4 me. I will be late, nearly 2am. Bt I will come . I promise. I will come whatever d conditions b. keep ur head cool. Don't let them know we r going 2 meet. Bye. Wait 4 me. Remember the sign of miss call will be turning the night bulb on. Keep ur window open. Luv u honey. Missing u badly sona... mmuuuaaahhhh."

No sooner had I sent the message, I got a call from mom.

"Hello.... What the hell I am hearing? Are you going to meet her? Are you out of mind?" mom yelled at me. I pretended not having heard her. What the hell is the network, it went wrong when, I wanted it to be alright. And now when I want it to perform in the same manner, it worked quite well. "Don't play pranks on me. I am your mother. I know you very well. Don't pretend that you are not getting me. Come on kid, say something. Show some courage."

"Sorry mom. How well you understand me!" I said.

"That's because I am your mom, and you are my child. You thought, you could make up everything with your dad, and I will not get any trace of it. I realized that, something was happening behind my back, when dad asked for your dress. And when Pooja called, everything become crystal clear. You two were trying to fool me!!!" mom said in a melancholy tone.

"Hey mom, please don't mind. Please. You know everything. Dad has nothing to do with this. He had also forbidden me, from going there. But he gave the permission ultimately when I requested him. I knew you will not allow me. So, I tried to hide the matter from you. Sorry mom. Ok. Now I am asking for your permission. Will you allow me to go there mom?" I asked her. I thought she would not say anything and will give me permission. But she gave me a cuff and then a straight smash in a knock out boxing match.

"You are not going there. If they get the slightest hint about you, what do you think they will leave you? You know them well. Don't you remember the days when they put you on wheel chair? They are very dangerous. Even the police officer is in their pay. You know everything and still want to go there? You are not going anywhere. You will be coming home directly, from the station. You may meet her tomorrow. You can't stop her from going away. What is the use of going there, so late in the night? Listen to my words carefully, you are not going there. Understand." Mom got angry while saying that.

"Are you finished? May I say something? I want to meet her at any cost. I know that, I am unable to change anything. But, this will give me at least some mental comfort. She is going away mom. Permanently. Do you think they will keep their promise? Never mom. Never. Think about her at least once. I have support, from you. I have friends, with whom I can laugh. She has nothing left to lose. I can't let her go away unhappy. I want to give her the last smile, at any cost. Please try to understand mom. Please." I requested humbly.

"No. I do not want to understand anything. Nothing. I don't want to think about her. I can only think about you. No one else. You will be in danger kid. Please listen to me. Hello...... are you getting my words Adi???" she asked.

But I did not have any answer. I just said, "Hell to the world. Mom, I am going to meet her. No one can stop me. Not even you. I will go and meet her even at the cost of my life. Ok... bye mom. See you soon," and cut the phone.

My next step was to call dad and let him aware of the situation.

"Hello. Dad. Mom knew everything. Pooja called and told her

everything. Where are you?" I asked.

"I knew it. Pooja's call came in front of me. Suddenly her tone changed and I fled. *Agar wahan rahta to, tumahri ma, mujhe katke, sukhake, mera achaar bana deti.* Now I am at the station. I can face anyone in the world, other than your mom. So, don't think about me." He said and laughed.

"Dad. Do you love me very much? Will you do something, I ask for? Dadddddd......" I asked.

"Why are you saying so? What do you want? Don't say that, you want me to return home. Please. I will do anything for you, other than that." He replied. Confusion was easily felt in his tone.

"Actually dad, I want you to return. She is alone. She will be angry, but I love mom very much. Only you can make her understand. Please dad, do it for me. Otherwise, she will feel hurt. Perhaps, she would come to station to stop me. Please dad go to her." I requested.

"You and your mom are the most freaked out personalities of the world. I am not going. Understand." Dad said. I got the sign, he emphasized on the word, 'understand', I knew that I had won the game, just away by a stretch, which would be over after saying 'please'. I did it and the game was won. Dad agreed to go to home and make mom understand the matter. I thanked the Almighty.

The train started going at full speed. I looked at the clock to find the time. It was 11.50 pm. Nearly an hour more to reach Chittaranjan. I looked out of the window pane, when by and by two messages came. I gazed at them to find that one was from mom and other was from Avishek.

"*Call me. I am sorry.*" Said the sms from mom.

"Hello. Ma. Why are you saying sorry? Its ok. You are right at your point and I am on mine. Dad is coming soon, perhaps reaching in five minutes. Keep your head cool and don't get angry with him. You understand naa…." I said.

"Ya sweetie. I got you. I understand everything. After you called off, I realized that I could ward you away from the whole world, but can not ward your heart away from everything. So, be safe dear. Maintain silence. Move secretly. Keep under cover." Mom said.

"Wait. Wait. Mom. What are you saying? I am going to meet my girl friend, not going in any war or some secret mission. Believe me, I will return safe. Nothing will happen to me. Your and dad's blessing are with me always. Ok. Bye mom. See you soon." I said and put the phone down.

I made a call to dad at once.

"Hello… where are you? Mom called. She had given the permission." I said jubilantly.

"What??? That's great. I am in Central Market. Bought a bouquet for your mom. But I must say, you two are the freakiest creatures of the world. Thank God, your brother is not like you or your mom. He is like me. If he had not been there, I do not know, how could I put up with you two. Whatever it is, leave it. I will be in station on time. Come soon dear. Ok. Bye." He said and put the phone down.

I looked at the other sms, which was from Avishek saying,

"*hi man. Ani returned. Exhausted. Saying he fucked the two. But I don't believe him. Tomorrow there is biochem class test. Without you, we are fucked up completely yaar. Everything seems like Hebrew. Ok. Bye. Have a safe ride. And, condom hai na?*"

I at once replied,

"*saale teri behan ki…, main edhar us se akhri bar milne ja raha hun, aur tu kamina chod ne ki baat karta hai. Fuck you kamina."*

Instantaneously I got another message from him.

"*why getting angry? Chillax. Take a chill pill yaar.sorry if I had hurt you."*

I replied, *"chill man. I m nt angry? And abt d tst, follow c2d theory, believe in urself. congrats ani instead of me, for finally fucking a girl. Bye."*

C2D Theory means, Co operate To Dominate Theory, extracted from the book 'FIVE POINT SOMEONE' by Chetan Bhagat. I read the story, and was so moved by the thought of group study that, I implemented it in my friend circle. And miraculously, all that worked. All five in the core group are star students of the class in respect of academic record. Even I got chance to sit for the Gold Medal exam, conducted by the college itself.

Amidst all these thoughts I noticed the low battery alarm on my mobile. I had got it completely charged before the journey, but so many phone calls and music through out the leisure told upon. I rose and went towards the end of the compartment. Thanks to the rail ministry, nowadays there are arrangements for mobile charging in the train. I put the mobile on charging and went to the sink to wash my face and get some refreshments.

My best friend, Sourav….

I waited for nearly 20 mins by the side of the train door for the mobile to get completely charged. By then the train had reached Asansol station. It was 12.50 then. The mobile showed, 'high' in charge column. I took it out. Then came out onto the platform and bought a packet of biscuits and a bottle of coke. I boarded the train again. Only four or five passengers had boarded the train in the station. It's the all time low passenger boarding I had ever seen in this station.

Suddenly I noticed that a sms had come. It was from Sourav. It said,

"*wats up buddy? Met her? Relax dude. Ur network is poor probably. So nt calling. C u soon. Gud nite.*"

I replied, "*no dude. Luck sucks man. Still in train, engine damage. I m getting nervous. Help me dude. Feeling very lonely man. Ok. Bye. Gud nite.*"

No sooner I had sent the sms, he called me.

"Hi. Where are you presently?" he asked.

"Asansol. Destiny fucked me up man." I replied.

"Leave all that dude. Why do you seem so depressed? Leave the whole matter in the hands of time. We are unable to do anything. Let the time play the role dude. Come out man. Don't get so frustrated. You have to accept it; it's been your destiny. You can't escape." Sourav said.

"But I can't man. I am trying to run away from the whole matter. But the more I am trying to come out of it; I am getting deeper in it. It's like quick sand, the more I am trying to get rid of it, it is engulfing me more and pulling me down." I said to him.

"I understand everything. I know it hurts a lot to get away from the person you love very much. I can understand the pain. I also had lost the person I once loved. Look at me, I still do not envy you, still we are good friends. I know these may hurt you, but forget her. Get on with the flow of life. You understand what I am trying to say. Please man, keep yourself intact." He urged in a low voice.

"The path had taken a sudden turn and I don't know the destination. I am losing everything dude. I am lost." I said in a pitiful urge.

"Don't ever talk like that. Think of the people who are dependent on you. You can't lose so easily. Its life man." He tried to console me.

"You are telling me to forget her???" I asked.

"Yuppp.... I am asking you to forget everything and get going in life." He said.

"Had you still been able to forget her? Tell me. Do you remember the filmy dialogue you always gave, '*when you first fell in love, did you put any condition that she would also feel for you? No naa..... Then how can you think of leaving your beloved? Love is very much like the life. Every stretch on its path does not give you happiness; there are bends in which you get only sorrow. Even then we don't stop to live. If that is so, how can you think of leaving your beloved.*' Don't you remember all that?" I asked him.

He was absolutely confused at such a shocking comment. He

resumed and said, "This is not the time for all this. You have gone mad."

"Ok. I am mad. But first answer of my question. Have you been able to forget her?" I questioned him.

"I told you to leave all this. Why are you digging out the old graves of the past? It's been nearly five years man. There is nothing to discuss any more." He responded.

"Don't try to distract me. Answer me. Had you still been able to forget her, after all these years? I want a clear cut answer. Come on speak out man. I have never asked you this. But today I want an answer." Our general conversation was getting heated. I don't remember the last time, when we had such a heated conversation.

"You are crossing the limits of my patience. Why do you want my answer? You want an answer in the affirmative, I am saying yes. Happy now?" his voice had risen up.

"Why are you getting so angry? I asked you a simple question. If there had been no feeling in your heart, you would have clearly said 'no'. But you kept nagging. You still love her dude. I know it and even felt it many a times. I had seen your love for Pooja in your eyes. You can hide your feelings in your heart. But your eyes always speak the truth. Someone had truly said that,

Only eyes speak the truth,
Neither the mirror nor the lips.
Only the person who loves you,
Can see the pain in your eyes,
While others will still believe in your smile.

Come on man, confess. I don't think we would again have the opportunity to have such a conversation again. Come on dude, say something." I lowered my voice.

He remained silent for a few seconds, then said finally, "Ya.... I still love her very much. I had not been able to forget her even after all these years." I felt the tremor his voice was getting.

"That's like my courageous friend. Then, you still have not been able to forget her. If that is so, how can you tell me to forget her so easily? You know everything, every condition and circumstances. How could you then expect integrity in my character? I can't dude. I can't." my voice got nearly choked with the severe headache I had.

"Ok dude, then..... Hello... are you getting me?" he asked.

"Ya I did get you hello."

"I can't hear you Adi. Can you hear me?"

Then the connection got broken. But I did not try to call him again. Neither did he. Perhaps we two were shocked, by the way the turn of the whole conversation.

The next moment I was completely lost in the memories of pain, solitude, and finally getting love. We three, Sourav, I and Pooja had been best friends from childhood. We had known each other, since class 2. We spent our childhood days together in the school and had great fun and were very happy. There were days, when one spent the day at the home of the other. Such was our friendship. But as we reached adolescence, everything changed. Both Sourav and I got attracted towards her. Sourav had guts and showed his affection to her. I was shy and always failed to make her realize that, I liked her. Whatever I did for her was taken as a gesture of friendship. I always wanted to sing a Bengali song to her,

Meye... tumi ekhano amai bondhu vabo ki,
kakhono ki amai vebechile bondhur cheye ektu khani beshi?

Naki vebe nebo ajo tumi amai cheno ni.

(Girl, do you still think me to be your friend only?

Had you ever thought of me, to be someone more than a friend?

Or else do I think that, you still had not recognized me?)

Finally I had to pay for my shyness. Sourav proposed to her and she said yes. She too had some sort of likings for him. The day when, Sourav told me about all that, I cried a lot. It was very painful. But somehow I managed to cope with everything, telling myself that, they were happy together and they were made for each other. I was not handsome compared to her. I was a big fat guy whereas he had a great physique. I transformed myself completely. But a few days after their relationship was formed, quarrels broke out between them due to his excessive possessiveness as well as difference in his way of thinking about everything. I had not talked to either of them regarding those matters. I had to suffer a lot due to them; I played the role of a bridge between them. It was always a confusing situation for me. One part of me wanted to increase the distance between them, but the other part said to sacrifice my feeling for my friend. But every time, friendship won the battle against love.

However, all my efforts to bridge the gap between them was in vain, when she clearly told him about her dislikes. He quarreled at that moment, but later on said 'sorry' and promised to change completely. But she did not give him a second chance. He was late by a couple of months. But the damage was done. She came closer to me in those days. Their connection was completely lost on by then. She realized my feelings for her, but she also got to know that I would never summon enough courage to propose her. She gave many hints and tried to encourage me to propose to her. But every time I made blunders. Finally she herself patched up with me. I must confess that, I still had not formally proposed to her.

Sourav tried to rectify all, but everything was lost by then. His relationship with both of us was spoiled. I tried to make it up, but the damage was irreparable. Finally he accepted everything after six months. We again became good friends and a few days later again best friends. But he snapped all relations with her. It was nearly a year later, they were on talking terms. And by the end of class XII, all relationships were resumed. She was my girl friend and he was my best friend. On the other hand, they too had become good friends. In those days he acted as bridge between us during small quarrels. We had a serious fight only once, but it had profound consequences in our relationship.

It was after the class XI annual exams. I went to my maternal uncle's home in Dhanbad. She was in her home. There in Dhanbad, I fell seriously ill with some sort of viral infection in the lungs. I was admitted to hospital. I sent many messages to her, but she did not respond to any of them. I returned home and called her. I told her about my illness, but she showed least attention to me. I felt very bad but said nothing. I did not call her for nearly four or five days. I was again admitted to hospital, with a relapse. But this time it was not serious. I was forbidden from talking due to pharyngitis. I made a message saying,

"Hi... wats up? Didn't ever wondered how I was? Didn't you even remember me once? Truly speaking, your behavior hurts."

She sent only a missed call after the sms. I got very angry with her behavior. I felt like crying out all my anguish. After two weeks we met and that was the first and last occasion when we two fought. Frankly speaking she had not quarreled, she had said nothing. It was me who shouted at her. We had met in the school playground.

I was kept waiting for nearly an hour that day. My temper knew no bounds with the passing time. Finally when she came I blasted her.

"Hi... How are you? Sorry for being late." she said.

"Oooooo... you are saying sorry!!! Had anything gone wrong with you?" I yelled at her.

"What? What do you want to say?" she asked in utter confusion.

"I just want to say that, you are getting more and more stubborn and arrogant day by day." I sparked out.

"Are you playing any pranks on me? If yes then stop it I say." She responded in a deep gurgling voice.

"That's the thing, 'I say'. Each and every time it is only you in the relation. Only you. Where is my place?" I shouted.

She finally lost her cool and shouted back, "Tell me what you want to say. There is no problem in my behavior. You are acting differently or better say over reacting."

"I hate this thing about you. You always think that whatever you do is correct. In the past, even from the hospital bed I messaged you. But you did not have the least consideration to ask me 'how are you'? At least I can expect this from you. But you never responded.

I again got admitted in hospital. The doctor advised me not to talk and take complete rest. Though I fled away from home, taking the mobile, only to talk to you. And you said, 'how could I know that you were ill? If you are taken to hospital twice in a week, it's not my duty to take information regarding you.' I cried that day, how could you say that to me. Every time, I call you, message to you, ask you about your exams, every day wish you 'good morning'. But even once, you do not reply in a heartfelt way. I am actually feeling neglected in the relationship".

"You said, that day, you got fought with Sourav, I must say, your this kind of arrogant behavior is the reason behind everything. You never want to look at the emotion of the other. You always seek attention, but never bother to give even a simple smile in return. Even if you had just simply said, 'how are you' once in that whole week, I would not have felt so hurt. I know that, your parents did not let you use the mobile, but don't you think that, if you really had wanted to talk, you could do it. But you did not. Your behavior had compelled me to wonder, what my place is in your life. I do not think you had missed me in the least in the whole period of two weeks."

"Mamun didi tells the truth. She says that, my over friendly behavior had decreased my importance in the life of others; everyone had taken me as an easily available thing. Make a missed call to him, he will call and talk to you for hours. Use him when you want and throw him out when you get bored. Is this the way you actually think about me???" I said and left the place, leaving here perplexed of the situation, not even turning to her, to see her reaction.

Money, the most powerful thing ....

"Excuse me, when is the train going to reach Jasidih?" The drunken person came to me and asked.

"I think it is going to take another couple of hours to reach Jasidih." I replied.

"If you don't mind, where are you going? Actually my reservation is in the waiting list. If possible, I would want to take your place." He said.

"I am going to Chittaranjan. Another half an hour, after the train would resume the journey. Oh... here the train starts now." I said and the train started.

"Wow. Chittaranjan. I spent my childhood days there. My father worked there in the Chittaranjan Locomotive Works. After I started working we shifted there. By the way I am in railway maintenance department. In which department do you work?" he asked.

I laughed a little and said, "You made a big mistake. My father works there, I am a college student. My dad is the Chief Electrical Fitter, in motor department. May I ask you a question?"

"Ya. Why not? You are from my home town. Ask, whatever you like?" he replied.

"So.. The RPF caught you. How did you get out of that? They behaved so rudely, and were seemed to be determined to put you in jail. How did you and the RPF boss came into settlement?"

The person chuckled a little and then started to speak, "Money, Money, my friend money. It's the most powerful thing in the world. I go by this train every week and I know the mentality of these duty men very well. They created a great fuss, saying that I was drunk completely and could create a problem for the other co passengers. It was just a show off in front of the passengers. They took me to the side, and threatened to take me to jail. But I gave them the thing they desired. I told them, that if they let me go, I will give them a thousand rupee note and the trick was done. They took the money and let me go. This is the real world; here if you have money, you can buy anything, even justice. I was asked to sit in the first class coupe, but it was very lonely there. So I again came here. Actually I do not like solitude. I fear loneliness. Whatever it be, whats your name and where do you study?"

"My name is Aditya. I study in R.G.KAR MEDICAL COLLEGE, Kolkata." I replied.

"Wow.... This means I am talking to a would be doctor. That's the noblest profession of the world. But never lose your inner self, never sell yourself to others. My younger brother is a doctor, from Patna. He earns a lot, but he always feels guilty for selling his soul to the medicine companies."

"Ya. I will comply with your wishes. Even dad says similar things." Before I could say anything further, his phone rang and he just moved out and went to the next coupe.

His words kept buzzing in my ears. He had actually spoken the truth. Money is the most powerful thing in the world, with that, one can buy even justice. I had seen an example of this principle in my own life. I looked out to see the darkness, and then compared it to the darkness within me. When the police had caught that man, I knew that he would certainly get freed. The dress of the man showed that, he comes from a rich background, and I knew that he would pay a lump sum of money as bribe and come out clean of all charges. I was then lost in the memories of the days when I was on a wheel chair.

I remembered the day, when I along with my father and lawyer, had gone to the local police station to file a case against Pooja's dad, an attempt to murder case. Nearly three months have passed, I was quite well then, but still on a wheel chair due to loss of all motor functions in the lower limbs.

When we entered the police station, we found that, the Officer in Charge was not there. We asked the constable about OC, to which he replied that, the previous day had been the birthday party of his son, and so he was going to be late. We were kept waiting. There were cells for different victims, but everyone was empty. Actually there is an almost peaceful environment all throughout in this area. I was fast losing my patience. Finally after one and half hours of waiting, the officer came. He came as a jet, and went away like a storm. He first glanced of us. Our lawyer, Mr. Arjun Bajwa, tried to tell him something, but he was in no mood to hear anything. He just asked him whether, it was an emergency case or not. That's all he said and disappeared like lightning sky. Two more hours had passed by then. I was feeling very unwell, but we had to wait to file the case. Prior to that, case had been lodged, but due to my absence on medical grounds, no step had been taken. We thought that, after my statement, the police would take appropriate step. Although dad was hopeful for justice, mom had said that all our efforts would go futile. She had said that, all the case had been set up by then. Finally when I was lost in thoughts, the officer stepped into the police station. I saw dad and Mr. Bajwa whispering to each other.

"Are you Ok son? Be cool and tell him everything confidently. Think before you say anything. Right kid?" dad asked me.

"I understand dad. Chill. I will do nothing wrong." I replied, but sorts of confusion and distractions was raging in their faces. After more 15 to 20 minutes, the officer came and occupied his seat.

"So, you came finally?" the officer looked at me.

"Hello sir. We are here, to file a case against Mr. Rajiv Malhotra, for sending goons and trying to kill my client, Mr. Aditya Verma." Said our lawyer.

"Excuse me. Let me talk to your client. So what do you think, is your lawyer is saying the same thing you want to say?" the policeman asked.

I just nodded to show that I agreed.

"But according to my knowledge, there was an attack on you and there were nearly ten goondas. It was dark and you were unable to see anyone's face. You had not reported any special feature of any criminal. Am I wrong in any of these? Isn't that the statement you gave in hospital to Kolkata police?" he asked in a firm voice. I was left with no other alternative, than to respond in affirmative to him.

"Then how can you say that, it was Mr. Malhotra, who had tried to kill you? He is a much respected person in this area. Do you have any proof? Do you understand, what I am saying? Your case does not stand even at a single point. You can not just blame anyone in such a manner." There was complete arrogance in his voice.

Suddenly, Mr. Bajwa lost his cool and spoke in some sort of higher pitch.

"Don't you think it is the duty of the police is to go out, collect all the possible evidences and find out, who the real person is, behind the crime actually? For your kind information, the goons once asked him about his girl friend, Pooja, daughter of Mr. Malhotra. He is against the relationship and had organized that attack to stop all these..."

"Don't teach me my duty. I know that it's the duty of police to catch the accused, if he or she had committed any crime. Here you have only allegation, not a single statement is based on reality. All that you are saying is only circumstantial. I don't think these allegations would stand even for a minute. There is no proof of the crime. We have nothing to do. Better have a settlement outside the court. It would be better for you. And if the case is taken to the court, then his girl friend's name would be involved. Many kinds of offensive questions will be asked about your relationship. Further the public would get a fresh, story to indulge in gossip. You know the common public, always loves to talk about such masala stories. What will be her position in the society? She would not be able even to keep her head up. Have you ever thought about all these things? " The officer said in a harsh voice.

"Excuse me sir.... You are trying to distract my client's attention." Mr. Bajwa rose from chair and got very angry.

"Hell to your excuse. I was not talking to you then. Who are you to interfere? And what do you think; your charge would stand in the court? Do you know, his lawyer is Surendra Banerjee! You are in no way comparable to him. He came here before you, and said that his client is clean in character and had no relationship with any criminals. And you Mr. Verma, why are you completely silent? Your son is taking the wrong path. Please, I request you to restrain him. You are making a big mistake." The OC said.

"Don't teach me what is right or wrong. I don't want any suggestion, from you regarding my son. So, how much money had he given to you?" Dad lost his patience and was getting completely out of control.

"What???" the police officer was furious. He came to dad and then dragged him by his collar and said, "I can put you all in jail, with the charge of verbally abusing an officer on duty. But, go away man; I do not want to have any talk with any of you. I do not want to get involved in any kind of controversy." He said.

"Sorry sir. Please do not mind. He just lost his temper. Please forgive him." Finally I spoke and requested him.

"Enough. Go away now. I was just telling you the right way to deal with the problem. I am not corrupt, but my seniors are. They have tied my hands regarding the case. I cannot help you in any way. Even later, you want to file any case regarding the incident; you are free to do that. I will never oppose you, but remember that all will ultimately be in vain. You can do nothing." He said and instantly got away out of the police station.

Suddenly the train stopped, again at a small station. I recognized it, Rupnarayanpur. It was like a 'outer' of Chittaranjan station. Most trains once stop there before getting into Chittaranjan. I took out my phone and called dad.

"Hello... dad it's me." I said in a loud voice.

"Ya kid. Where are you? Mom and I are at the station." He replied.

"What. Mom has came! I told you not to bring her." I said.

"Chill son. Everything is ok. Where are you?" Dad asked.

"At Rupnarayanpur station."I replied.

"Hey, talk to Mom." Dad said.

"Hello sweetheart. I am waiting for you. Don't think I am here to stop you. I love you dear. Come sharp kid." Mom said.

"Sorry again Mom." I told mom.

"Don't be son. I should have understood you. Came sharp." Mom said.

"How could I mom, until the train starts on its own. I do not want to run either, let the train start and I will be there. Bye Mom." I laughed and disconnected the phone.

A few minutes later the train reached the destination. I took my luggage and came out. Mom and Dad were standing near the overhead bridge. I waved to them.

"Hi..." I said and then hugged them. "So. I am here now. Have you brought food? I am dying to eat something. Hungry Mom....."

"Lets go to the car son. Arun is waiting there with your cycle. Your dinner is in the car. Your favorite, paratha and alu ki sabji, with rosogolla." Mom said and we walked to our car, which was parked outside the station.

Chittaranjan station ....

"So a tough journey indeed. Bad luck son. Take your food and get ready quickly." Dad said.

"It's been a bad journey. Never faced such a situation ever before. What can we do, it was a mechanical fault. That's it... you can't escape what is written in your fate." I replied.

"Hey bro. how are you doing?" I asked my younger brother, Arun who had come with my cycle.

"Yesterday you asked the same question. I was fine yesterday and so I am today. It's been old way to greet. You are pathetic. You have become old mannered." He replied. Actually he studies in a boarding school in Dehradun, and is mere in sync with the latest mindset. Typically foreign mode of temperament. He always thinks us to be old fashioned freaks. But he is a nice chap. Likes to talk straight, always tells the truth, and faces everything. Likes to hear hard metallic English music and slow sentimental Hindi songs.

"Don't start again. Ok. Give me a hug boy." I said and he leaped at me.

"Bhaiyaa, you are going to meet Pooja Didi? Good luck. Mom is really worried about you. Have a talk with her. Love you Bhaiyaa." He said.

"And when did you come here? Mom had not told that you were coming. Even yesterday, you had not told me that you were coming." I asked him.

"Ya, just wanted to give you all a surprise. You said that, you are going to meet her for the last time most probably. Then how can I stay there? I came just to meet you. Took an early morning flight today to Kolkata and from there straight home by Balia Express. Dad was dumbstruck when he saw me at the dinner. When he had came, to take your dress, he had not seen me. And when he returned, his face was worth watching." Arun said and laughed a lot. Dad too joined him. But I noticed that mom was standing still.

"Hey Mom, why are you standing still? Are you still angry with me? Please Mom, don't be angry. Try to understand me Mom. Please." I requested. But she remained silent. She entered the car, I followed her.

She unpacked for the dinner. She gave plates to Dad and bro. then served us food. But she did not take anything.

"Why are you not taking anything? I told you na... please forgive me. Don't be upset. You gave permission on phone, then why are you showing this attitude now? You are hurting me Mom." My voice trembled.

"Who am I to be angry with you? You belong to us no longer. You now belong to someone else. That's it. I thought you were my son you would care for my feelings. But alas! You had moved a long distance from us." Mom threw the words at me in a crimpy low pitched voice.

"What the hell are you saying mom? You are now creating a scene.

Why are you saying all this stuff? The matter was settled over the phone." I said.

"Yes, there is no point in saying these things to him. You accepted what he said. Don't pretend to be dumb. Why are you bluffing?" dad nearly scolded.

"Why are you coming between us? Please understand my condition. You are his father. You can feel free. But I can't. I have given birth to him; I have him brought up to this age. I had almost lost him in the past. I can't take it any more. Please try to understand my mental state and think about it afterwards." Mom said and started to cry.

"Why are you behaving in this manner Mom? Bhaiyaa will be alright. He is your brave son Mom. Don't you believe him? That incident occurred only due to the fact that, he was unaware that, they could do anything like that. Come on mom. Don't do this." Arun told Mom.

I patted him on the back. But she was still crying incessantly. I got very confused. The dilemma was taking its hold on me. My stomach nearly gurgled and I rushed out of the car and vomited. I had severe headache. My head seemed to be going round and round like a spinning top. I was completely startled by the situation, which was going out of control with every passing second.

"Are you Ok, sweetheart?" Mom rushed to me. "That is the reason I do not want to let you go there. You arrived after a long journey. You require rest. Come kid. Hurry up. We gotta go home."

"Sorry Mom. I am not going with you. I have promised her and I have to keep that promise. I must go and meet her. You are saying that, I am coming after a long journey, but do you realize that she is going on a never ending journey, a few hours later. I am saying na, I will be alright and would be back home safely. Why are you acting in that way? Am I a school going kid? I am twenty now Mom. Please let me take the decision. Don't interfere." I said in quite a loud voice. In reply she started to cry again. I turned toward Daddy and signaled him to make Mom understand.

Dad went to her and took her in arms. He wiped the tears streaming down her eyes and said, "Take it easy dear. Our kids have grown up. Let them do whatever they want."

Mom blasted on Dad saying, "I know that they are grown up, but they are still our children. We can't let them take to wrong path."

"You should have thought of this earlier." I said from the side.

"Shut up Adi, or I will give you a tight slap. You are not going anywhere other than home at this time. Understand?" Mom shouted.

"Then what about that you said on phone?" I asked.

"I beg pardon for saying all those things. I was just carried away by emotions. I am sorry for that. 0k. now let's go home." Mom said.

The environment was getting heated up. Both mom and I were on fire. It's been years when we exchanged such heated conversations.

"I will go Mom. You can't stop me. Even if you cry to stop me, I will still go. I am Dad's worthy son. I do not fear anything. And you talk about, risks of love!!! If Dad had not shown the courage to flee with you and marry you, then we would not be here with you?" It was my time to blast. "I am not fearful like you. I will go Mom. I will go." No sooner I had shouted at Mom and she hit over me. She gave a tight slap on my cheek, the hardest ever.

"Ok. Do whatever you want, but never ever call me Mom again." She said and after coming out of the car, she started to walk towards the darker alleys.

"Hey Mom. Sorry. I never meant to hurt you." I shouted. But only saw a few faces turning towards us on the station road. Dad came to me.

"I am sorry Dad. Believe me, I never wanted to hurt her, but things just came out. Forgive me Dad. I made a blunder. Sorry Dad." I apologized.

"Its ok Adi. If I had been you, perhaps I would have done the same thing. Don't worry son. Go and get her. Why are you laughing?" he turned towards Arun.

"Its nothing. I just laughed.... I just smiled at the way you talked." He said in a jubilant mood, as such nothing had occurred there.

"It does not seem to be a matter which you can poke fun at. There is nothing to laugh at. It was just a man to man talk." Dad said to him.

"Sorry dad." Arun said.

"You should be, dear. Adi go and grab Mom. She is not far away. Best of luck. She is waiting for you. Go my son." He said to me and then went to bro. In the meantime, while I changed my T shirt and was taking some water, I heard something weird from Dad. He was talking to Arun.

"Kid you are grown. Its time I must talk to you. Do you love anyone? Do you love any girl like your elder brother?"

"On one hand you are saying that I have grown up, and on the other you are calling me 'kid'!!! I had told you many a times not to call me 'kid'? Why don't you understand? And to your question, my answer is no. I don't have any girl friend. I always mess up with gals." He replied. I laughed a bit.

"Ooooooo. Don't say that. Your brother too messed up with girls and now he runs after girls. Leave it. I just want to say that, if you fall for a girl, first enquire if her dad is stubborn or arrogant. Without such material, your love life will be boring." Dad said. At this I could not control my laughter. I looked at the road and found Mom sitting on a culvert. I turned to Dad and said, "You are the best Dad of the world. I love you Dad. Bye. I will be back within minutes."

I ran to Mom. She was sitting still and did not bother to look at me.

"I am sorry Mom. I never intended to hurt you." I said and sat beside her. I took her palm over mine and said, "Will you not forgive me? Please Mom? I beg pardon. Pleaseeeeeeee."

"Ok. Ok. I don't want any more acting. Enough. You need not to say sorry. Rather, I must say sorry to you. I should not have bluffed you. I thought, if I could restrain you in the train, but impose pressure after you arrive here, I could stop you from going there. Sorry for being so mean to you."

"Why are you saying such things Mom? Whatever you had done it was all for my benefit. You are the best Mom of the world. I love you Mom. Oh … yes, Mom I had once written a poem on you. Its in my mobile. I want to recite it for you. The poem goes like this,

You are the person, who brought me in to this world.
You are the person, who brought me up in this human society.
You are the person, who waited for me all the time, when I was out.
You are the person, who remained ready to hand me a glass of water, when I came from outside.
You are the person, who loves me the most in this world.
I love you Mom. I miss you.

How was that? Actually I have some thing more to say. I put on the music in the mobile and played a song from the movie, '*Rab ne bana di jodi.*'

Na kuch pucha, Na kuch maanga,
Tune dil se diya jo diya….
Na kuch bola, Na kuch tola,
Muskurake diya jo diya….
Tuhi dhoop, tuhi chaaon,
Tuhi apna paraya….
Aur kuch na janun, baas itna hi jaanun,
Tujh main rab dikhta hai,
Yaara main kya karun…..

I love you more than anyone else on this earth Mom, even more than her. But she is waiting for me. I have to go mom." I said.

"Ok son, go. This time I am speaking from the heart. Go, get her. May God be with you. Don't forget that they are very dangerous kind of people. Don't create a scene and try to be quiet. Switch your mobile off. In these type of mission, mobiles act as homing device. Whatever it be, she is going away tomorrow. Let her go in peace. In the evening, when she called, she was crying. Be careful son. I will pray for you. I will pray for your love. I love you my son." She said and held my head in her hands, then pulled me towards her, and then kissed on my forehead.

By that time, we reached our car. Dad and Arun were standing there, probably quarrelling over Manchester United, a world famous football club.

Then I took my cycle and said a good bye to all of them. I found them driving back in the car; the car had some kind of starting problem. But finally after 5 mins of trying, the car started and they went away.

"Good bye Bhaiyaa. I will be waiting for you at home. Come sharp." Arun shouted.

In the way to her home ....

I rode on the cycle and proceeded towards her home, which was nearly 20 – 25 mins away. I looked at the watch, and it showed 1.55 AM. Suddenly out of the blue, I remembered the promise that I had made in the hospital, when I had met her last time. Red roses. I had completely forgotten the matter.

I thought that I would ask Dad to bring flowers to the station, but Mom's and Sourav's call made me completely crazy. At such fag end of night, it was impossible to buy a bouquet from any shop. But to me, word is law. So I decided to go to the central market and look for some shopkeeper, sleeping outside his shop. I looked at the purse, there were 550 rupees in it. I decided to pay, whatever he would ask for just to have the flowers. I turned my cycle, and started to move as fast as I could. That moment, I realized that if I had known driving, I should not have to face these problems. But the next moment, I realized that, if I went to her home, by bike or car, silence could not be maintained.

I reached the flower market in less than 10 mins, but did not find a single shopkeeper, sleeping outside. I looked through all the shops, but the whole place was deserted. I questioned myself, 'how can I be such a fool?'. But I was determined to get flowers by any means.

All the flower shops were installed on cement basements. No guard at all. All the bouquet and flowers were kept over the basement, sprinkled with water. They were covered by a plastic sheet and tied up. I always wonder how they keep the flowers intact, without any refrigerator in the shop. That day I understood that the shopkeepers applied some kind of chemical, for freshness.

I thought for a few moments and then got down from the cycle. Entered such a shop and quickly loosened the ropes. Slowly I ripped the plastic cover and the first bouquet I touched was made up of rose. I was more than happy after getting the flowers. I could not make out the color of the flowers, but by the light of the mobile I confirmed that, they were roses. I took the bouquet and put it in the bag.

After that, I opened my purse and took the five hundred rupee note. Then I cut a page from my diary, and in the light of the mobile, wrote on it,

"*mujhe phool ki bahut jarurat thi, isi liye aise chor ki tarah le ke ja r aha hun. Par main koi chor nahin, isi liye yeh chithi aur 500 rupay rakh r aha hun. Is se sayad apka sab nuksan bhar jayega.*"

No sooner I had came out of the shop, than I heard the whistle of the night guards approaching towards me. I made least sound and come out of the shop.

"Holy shit." I said to myself as the night guards had already been on the road on which the shop was. Any attempt to flee would be seen by them, and I would be caught. I approached the cycle, which was kept parked by the side in the shadow of the shop. I put it down and hid myself behind the shop. And I tried to keep quiet. My pulse quickened; I was actually thrilled as well as frightened by the sudden change of situation.

A few minutes ago I had thanked my luck for getting the flower, but now I was blaming my luck for always putting me in bad circumstances. The guards stood in front of the shop and one asked the other for *khaini*. The other quickly obliged.

"Hey what is that? Something seems to be shining in the dark." one of the guards said to the other.

I realized quickly that they must be approaching my cycle. Instantly I took a stone from the ground and threw it directly towards the shutter of a distant shop.

"Bang" there was a loud sound.

"Who is there?" the guards shouted and ran towards the closed shop to see what the matter was.

I came out of hiding. In my hurry, I fell down. It did not hurt me much, just a simple pain in the hand. But the actual damage was done. There was a large sound as I had shouted 'ahhh' while falling down. That was enough to attract the attention of the guards. They came towards me shouting, "Who the fuck is there?" I quickly took my cycle, rode it and paddled as fast as I could.

"Stop. Stop there I say." One of them shouted, but I was not an insane to stop at the shouting. I drove at my highest possible efforts. They ran after me. Suddenly someone throw a stone attempting me, but I missed it by an inch. The next moment I took a right turn, and the road was down hill type. My speed knew no bounds and I escaped narrowly.

I thanked the Almighty, for the close shave.

"How many surprises had you kept for me this night?" I uttered looking at the moonlit sky full of stars.

On the side of the dam ....

I came to her home. It was 2.40 am on clock. I gave her a missed call. But the night bulb was not put on. Again I gave a missed call, now for a full call time. This time few moments later she put on the night bulb. I got my sign.

Slowly and quietly I entered their boundary. She lives in a mansion like house, which is single storied (as it was a government house). It had nine or ten rooms. She lives in the southernmost corner of the house, the direction, the breeze from the dam always blows. The room opens into a verandah and on the sides there were the drawing room and kitchen. So the sounds from the room is heard by none. Only this aspect of the room's location had supplied me the courage, necessary to infiltrate twice on her past birthdays, once after the exams, once after passing the senior secondary board exam. But today as I was crossing the garden, the small fountain, the culvert, many past memories were coming back and forth.

Those days were pretty good, adventurous and joyous. But this day, everything, even the smile from the core of the heart was missing. Everywhere there was a scream. On those days, silence seemed to be a weapon for the purpose of infiltration. But today, silence and darkness, seemed to engulf all my senses. Each and every thought of happiness seemed to be blacked out. A grey and glum atmosphere was surrounding me. All my senses were getting submerged in the melancholy tune of solitude. All this started after I entered the house. Each and every object was impacting me with the memories attached to them. In class five, when I had come to her house for the first time with Sourav on a rainy day, we had floated paper boats on the fountain. On her birthday, when for the first time, I went to her place, I gave her flowers from the garden, not knowing exactly what the flower was. Memories kept floating and restricting my path. 'But I have to go to her, she must be waiting', I said to myself and controlled my thoughts.

I came to her window pane. "Pooja. Pooja..." I uttered in a low voice and patted the window pane. Suddenly I heard some footsteps and I lowered my head. Few minutes later, she opened the window. The window was made of glass, without any iron beams.

"Hi... come out. Let's go to the dam and sit there. Come out." I said in the lowest possible pitch.

"Wait." She said and went back and locked the door from inside. There after, she took a box and came out. I wondered about the box, but I was not in mood to indulge in any such foolish talk standing there. As the window was nearly five feet high, she said, she would jump out of it. I told her, not to do that.

"Come. Hug me." I said standing below the window pane. "I will take you to the ground." She laughed a bit after hearing such. But, she did exactly what I had said. The next minute, we were both on the ground.

The breeze from the south was cool as ever. There was an absolute silence reigning all around. Only some night birds were hooting from time to time. We came out of the gates slowly. Then, we increased our pace and reached the side of the dam.

We sat down at our favorite spot. A gulmohur tree by the side of the dam, with a cement culvert all around. Although, the place was near her home there was no chance of being spotted. One had to cross a playground to reach the spot. That was the reason, it was a safe place. The school playground has always been my first choice, for meeting. But she says, the distant horizon of water, that touches the gulmohor tree is very charming.

I took the mobile out to check the time. It showed five minutes past three. After that, I took out the bouquet and knelt in front of her. Then started the music, '*Zara si dil main de jagah tu*' from the latest hindi blockbuster movie 'Jannat'.

"Pooja, I have never said this to anyone. But I want to say this to you. You are the only person in this world, to whom I can say this. You are the only person, whom I loved, I love, and I will love for ever. I love you. I love you Pooja. You are always in the deepest thoughts of my heart. You are everything in my life. Will you please step into my life and fulfill my incomplete life? Will you be mine?" I proposed to her for the first time.

In the dim moonlight, I was able to see the tears in her eyes clearly. I was still kneeling down. She sobbed a little, and came down to me.

"I do. I love you too Adi. You are my life Adi. You are the only reason, for which I breathe, live this life and of course still believe in love. I am always yours. I have been dying for this day, when you would propose to me. I knew that, you will someday, but never knew that, it would be at this fag end of everything." She said and tears rolled down to her lips.

I went near her and hugged her tightly. We stood up. She cried incessantly. Even my heart sank, but somehow I controlled myself. But the environment affected on us profoundly. The dim moonlight, cool breeze, the deep injury in the heart compelled our emotions to burst out. The next moment we were engaged in a lip lock. I was in a state of utopia, where there is no problem, no sorrow, only happiness. After many minutes snogging each other, we finally parted. She was still in tears. Even I was in tears at heart, not showing externally, but I was completely shattered and broken.

I resumed, "So I finally proposed to you and said 'I love you' in the style you wanted. Do you remember the time, when you said me that you love me? I was a bit shocked after hearing that. It's the same place na.... the place is same, the persons concerned are same, but only the time is different." I laughed a little.

There was a slight bending in her lips. She smiled a bit too and said, "How can I forget that day? Ya.. The time is completely different. That was morning at 7 or 8 am and its mid night now. Those were the loveliest days of my life. Everything was colorful, everything was beautiful. But now everything has changed. Now....." before she could say anything more, I restrained her from diving in the past memories, which were beautiful.

"Your face was worth watching. When you said that. You have feelings for me, *ekdam rodlu face banaya tha.?*" I tried to lighten up the moment a bit.

"Why should my face not be pathetic? You were a dumbo from the beginning. Its always the matter or better say concern of boys to propose to girls. But, here I have to propose to you. You knew that, I loved you after the break up, though you could not gather enough courage, to ask me. Ufff. My sweet dumbo." She said.

"No. That is not true. I thought of proposing to you, but before I could say anything, you came to me. Actually after your break, I was confused whether you would like anyone. Ok. Leave it." I tried to save myself.

"Why should I leave you? You are trying to fool me. I know you very well. Its been years since we have been together. You would never get the courage to come and say that 'I love you'. You always feared that, I might leave you and even break the friendship. You have always been a blunder with girls. Even in the class, you could not talk to any girl freely, other than me. Am I wrong?" she charged me.

I was left with no other alternative, than to comply with her words. Actually she was telling the truth. Girls can never think of the situation a boy faces, when he has to propose to a girl. These sentiments are beyond the girls to understand. When a boy goes to propose to a girl, a number of thoughts encircle his mind. What if she refuses you, what if she slaps you, what if she says get out, what if she snaps all relationship .....? What if... What if ... What if ... Ufff... There are a lot of things. And on the other hand, when a girl proposes, she had already won 90 percent battle. She could fail, if and only if she is least liked by the boy concerned. Girls propose only when they knew that, the boy will never turn her down.

"Hey... where have you been lost?" she asked.

"Just remembering the way you proposed." I said and started to imitate the manner, in which she talks. "Adi... will you answer my question? Whom do you love? Is she in our class? Do you like me? Will you be my love? Blaa... Blaa... Blaa..." I teased her.

She got angry and said, "Stop this I say. I never said that. And you are saying that, you had not given any clear cut answer then. You were completely confused."

"What are you saying? Now you are talking like a mad person. I kissed you on your cheeks. In which better way, could I have given you the answer? You always have problems with my attitude. You always think that, I am good for nothing." I said and showed annoyance.

"Oh... hoooooo..... My sweetheart is angry!" She kissed my cheeks and we were again engaged in a tight hug. But this time it was a much tighter embrace. Each and every inch of our body was getting caressed. It was not a sexual hug, but a formal tight hug, in some different manner, with deep affection, carried out with the loveliest emotions of the world. It was just the, bursting out of a dormant volcano. A reign of silence ruled our senses for the next few minutes.

She broke the silence in an unprecedented as well as unexpected way. She opened the box, which she was carrying. To my utter astonishment, the box contained all the gifts, cards presented by me to her on different occasions. These were holding within the memories of the most beautiful days we spent together. She had also brought a torch. Now she switched it on.

"These are the best memories of our life. I do not know where they would be tomorrow. I want you to keep all these ~~as the~~ memento of our love. I know I would never return. But I still want to keep all these safely. I want to keep all these stuff with me, but they will never allow me to keep these. Yesterday they found out this box and threw it in the dust bin. I collected it from there. The memories associated with them will always be in my heart and soul. Please take this." She said and handed over the box to me.

I took the box from her hand and then opened it. The first object I took out was a small teddy bear. I had presented that on her birthday.

"Do you remember this? It's my first gift to you na?" I asked and she smiled a little. "I can never forget this. That day you kissed me for the first time. I still get goose bumps whenever I think about that day. I must say, that day gave me the most erotic moment of my life. It was completely unbelievable for me that, in reality, some girl is kissing me. I can still taste that birthday cake. In the backyard of the school, after the classes, only you and me. We cut the cake, and you took a piece in your mouth, half part outside. Then gestured me to take it directly and we kissed. It was very much immature type, but I love that sensation. I must confess that, when you signaled, I was shell shocked by the thought. Back home I asked myself, whether I had done it in reality or it was a dream. You are always forward in all senses in our relation."

"If you liked it so much, you should have told me it earlier. I would definitely arrange for a cake, to be taken by us together." She said and laughed.

She then took out a piece of paper, nearly torn. She said, "Hey have a look at it. This is your first love letter. Do you remember what you had written in it?"

"Truly speaking, sorry dear, I do not remember anything about that. The thing I remember is that it was an mix of some Enrique songs." I replied.

"Yup... you are right. It was a letter fully extracted from English songs. After that you have never ever written a letter to me.

"Why should I write after that? Both of us got our personal mobile phones, and that's it. No need of letters remained. Though letter writing had always been liked by me, I prefer mobile as well as orkut messaging. Even shorter than e mails in language. Click a button and you reach your desired person." I said.

"Were you lazy from childhood, or have become such after becoming a *taal ka jhar*?" she asked in a joking manner.

"I think, after I met you. I thought we would be together and you will do all my works. So become lazy day by day. And now I am an embodiment of laziness." I said.

Like a sudden bolt of lightning, the smile on her face vanished. I realized that I had touched the wrong chord. I should not have mentioned that. I quickly took out a card from the box.

"That is our first valentine day card, right?" I asked.

"Wow... You remember it all." She asked still in a gloomy tone.

"Why should not I dear? It was a gift to my lady love. I remember each and every moment related to you. And this card specially. Uncle caught you with this card after your aunty spilled the beans. How did you still manage to get it?" I asked.

"I stole it from papa. You were always right about aunty. You had always told me, not to tell her everything. But I ignored your words and that's why the conditions are what they are. I wish, I had listened you, and ..." she could not continue and started crying.

I touched her lips and put my finger on them. "Sshhhh. Why are you crying for the past? Past is past. Don't think about those things. We can't bring back time, so there is no point to cry remembering the mistakes we made. Leave those things aside. Stop crying or I will go." She stopped sobbing.

"Promise me you will not throw it away. I know my chances of return are very few. But I still believe in God and the miracles He does. I give you free pass. If in these days, someone comes in your life, then I request don't let her go. You are free from my side. Just keep these things; it would be everything for me." She said. Her voice nearly crumpled. She closed the box and kissed it.

"What the hell are you talking? You will return dear. Believe me. Everything will be fine. I will definitely bring you back. And about the free pass, I must say, 'no thanks, I don't require them'. I can't love anyone else, other than you. If I had to marry someday, then either it would be you or someone of my parent's choice. I can never love other than you." I said to which she just exclaimed, "Uufffff. How romantic!!!!!"

She further added, "Why are you trying to fool me? It's only me, who always guards you from other girls. If I had not restricted your mixing with other girls, you would certainly have left me by this time. Sneha, Sanjana, Mausam, the three most beautiful girls of our class fell for you. But I won the jackpot. Whatever it be, you are always been a ladies man. I don't know how every girl, who comes near you falls for you. You are smart, but lack looks as well as charisma."

"I can't understand, whether you are saying that I am good or saying that I am bad or likewise. I have never fallen for any girl other than you." I said in disgrace.

"Leave it. So how is your filthy college bitch?" she asked.

"Who? Whom are you talking of?" I asked.

"Trishna... don't you remember her? To my knowledge she never misses a single chance to woo you." She said.

"Stop this nonsense. She is just a friend. I do not have any feelings for her. And stop calling her 'bitch'. She is a friend indeed." I said.

"Woooo. The lover boy gets hurt. I wonder about you. After my departure, you would be completely free to do anything. You are a boy after all. You will certainly fall for her, after sometime. Look in your mailbox, it contains mine and her messages in at least 1:10 ratio." Her voice seemed frustrated. I realized that, she was talking all this nonsense just to relieve herself of the immense pain, she had been feeling. So I did not respond rudely, rather tried to keep myself cool.

"Ya. I think you are right. I think I must say yes to her proposal. She is damn sexy after all. Everyone in the college falls for her. Now when you are gone, I would be at free will. I would have no bondage and perhaps make her my new girl friend. She is very rich too. I would not have to pay any bills, she will call me every time, what I had to do, is to give her only a missed call." I said and instantly she got angry.

"Hey sona don't be angry. I was just joking. It was you, who started all this. Ok leave it. Arindam came na?" I asked her.

"Yup. He came in the afternoon. He is going to Delhi with us. Bhaiyaa would load all the luggage on the train, and auction the furniture today at 4 pm. He would come by air the next day. You know, once that chap came to talk to me. But I behaved very rudely. Mom scolded, but I was happy. Indeed he needs that type of treatment." She said in a jubilant tone.

"You should not be so rude to him. After all he is your would be husband........" I laughed.

"I will kill you if you ever say this. I will die rather than marry him." She said arrogantly.

"Ya. But I must say, he loves you very much. It is 100 percent definite that, you hold a very special position in his heart. If it had not been true, why should he still want to marry you, after knowing everything about our relationship? He is a nice guy. He has everything, family status, good economic background, everything. He will certainly keep you happy. He is ideal for you. I am completely unsuitable for you as your life partner, in looks as well as passion.

Most importantly your parents love him. You would not have to fight with any one." My voice trembled.

"Love my foot. He only loves my dad's property. Nothing else. His parents are minding money. He knows nothing but money. He wants to marry me, for the 10 crore ancestral properties I owe. And you are saying that, he will keep me happy. I must say, I can never be happy with anyone other than you. My condition is pathetic dear. I can't express it in words." She said and I noticed the tear drops that were streaming down.

"What do you think, only your condition is pathetic? Mine is too dear. It… it seems that, I am standing in a long completely dark tunnel, with one of my feet entangled in the rail line going through the tunnel. I can not go forward or turn back. I was left there to find the time when the train would come and rip me into pieces. I wonder, whether the train would strike me from the front or the back." The wall of my emotions finally got shattered and tears streamed down my cheeks.

"Hey. You were telling me not to cry. Now why are you crying yourself? Stop it I say. I can't bear it. Otherwise I will start to cry too. Stop I say…." She ordered.

"I am not crying. Perhaps something had gone into my eyes." I replied in haste. I knew she had definitely identified my bluff, but who cares as she did not respond.

Again a silence filled the environment. I stood up. Instantly, she pulled my hand and pulled me down, then she kissed me on the forehead and we hugged each other again.

"I want to ask you something. Please tell me the truth. What did dad say when he met you? I was in hospital then, you went away without meeting me. After that we only met once at Dev's elder sister's marriage reception party. Over the phone neither I nor you ever talked on that matter. You once told me about some kind of conditions, put to you. What are they? What is the game plan of Dad?" she questioned.

I said, "It's been one and half months ago, when you were in hospital. But I still remember each and every detail clearly."

My meeting with her dad ....

As soon as I entered your house, Sheela Mousi came out as if as she had been waiting there for me. She took me in and asked me take a seat on the sofa in your Dad's reading room. I waited for nearly 10 – 15 minutes, when a number of thoughts came to my mind. Once I thought of venting all my anger on him, but I restrained myself thinking that, he might have changed at heart, and is feeling sorry for the incidents of the past. The next moment I thought, can a person like him, could really change?

"Excuse me Aditya Babu. Do you want to take tea or coffee or cold drink?" Sheela mousi asked.

"No thanks. I don't want any of them. I am alright. Where is uncle? Is he out of home?" I asked the maid.

"He is in the bathroom and madam has gone for some grocery shopping. They will be coming soon. I was told that you would be coming, and to take good care of you." She said and asked me whether, she could resume her household work. I nodded and she went away, to do her household work.

On the table there was a '*India Today*' magazine. I went through the pages in a hurried manner, but found nothing interesting in it. Actually my mind was somewhere else whereas my body was someplace else. My soul was roaming about freely in the ocean of thoughts.

'What did he call me for?' was the question that was stirring my each and every sense. I had never thought of something like this, him, accepting my relation with her daughter and letting us to be together. There was no point thinking that, it was unlike has nature. It was a logical thought. But the heart was saying that, perhaps he had changed.

There was a constant battle when Pooja's dad finally arrived.

"Hello young man… how are you? Did Sheela take good care of you?" he asked and extended his hand towards me.

We shook hands. "Hello uncle. She offered me drinks, both hot and cold. But I refused. She made me feel perfectly at home."

"Ohhhhooooo. Pardon she had not put on the a.c. even in these scorching hot days. Sorry Aditya, I better put on the a.c. You would feel completely comfortable then." He said and went for the a.c.

Instantly I said, "It is ok uncle. I am fine. I don't need the a.c. The fan is fine and I am feeling absolutely comfortable."

"Oh yes, I had completely forgotten that you don't have air conditioner in your house. You have fans only, that is the reason for which, you are not used to it. But I can not tolerate this scorching heat any more. I better turn it on." He said to me.

I got the first blow straight. I had never thought that, he would say something like that, on this day. He was just disrespecting me and my family in an oblique manner. He had done that many times earlier. But I got the signal. He had not changed even slightly. I got ready to take such blows, which were inevitable. I recognized the same filthy laugh, he always had. I understood, he had not changed even an inch. He was the same person, who always thought that, he was the most superior person of the world.

"You seem to be thinking something. May I know what you are thinking?" he said and sat on the easy chair in front of the sofa.

"Nothing important uncle. I was just thinking about your last words. Actually if I and my brother don't have the problem of tonsillitis, we would certainly have bought an ac or had made our home centrally air conditioned." I chuckled a little, as I knew he too had never dreamt of any repartee.

"Ufff. It seems you have taken my words to heart. You know my nature. It always happens to me. I wanted to mean something else, and end up meaning a completely different thing. Sorry, if I have hurt you in any sense. You know me very well, I can never think of hurting you, even in my wildest dreams. Surely Aditya, I never intended to insult you." He mumbled.

I just said to myself, "Fuck you. If you had not been older, I would certainly have given you a tight slap. Not in you dreams, but in reality, you had sent goons to beat me up. It was your bad luck and my good luck that I fucked up all your planning." I just wanted to say it loudly and slap him for all the wrong he had done to me and Pooja. But the moral teachings of my mom and dad restricted me from doing any such thing.

"So, now I want to directly come to the reason, for which I had called you here. But before that, I insist you to take some coffee or tea. Please." He said in a wicked manner.

"Ok. I would like to have coffee. I never take tea, I don't like the taste." I replied.

"Well. Fine. Sheela, make two coffees. Fast." He shouted.

"So how are your parents? Your brother is in 11th, right?" he asked and I replied just saying, everything is fine.

"How are the studies going on? I guess, very well. I heard about you from Pooja, you stood first in the college in the last semester."

I just nodded and said, "College and studies are going superb. No problem in anything. Everything is just moving fine."

"That is very good. You must become a very good doctor one day. You must be your parents' proud. I just want to say, please be gentle and kind to the poor and distressed people. They need persons like you, who are really good at heart, who do not look at this profession just as a good way of making money. You should........oh, here cornes Sheela with coffee. Please have coffee."

Sheela mousi handed over the coffee cup to me. I looked at the person, sitting just opposite to me. I wondered, how could a man with such monster like nature, say such good things. I took my first sip, when he blasted the first bomb at me.

"You are well aware of the situations, which had compelled me to meet you. My nature is completely known to you. I hate beating about the bush. I believe in talking everything clearly, straight forward. So, without wasting your as well as my valuable time, I want to come to the point directly. Do you get it?" Asked Mr. Malhotra.

"Ok. I get it. That is fine. It is always better to say everything clearly, keeping nothing secret. I always believe in this mode of personality and always try to follow this type of mentality." I nodded. I put down the cup, and turned round to find aunty approaching.

"Oh. Here comes her Mom. Take a seat. So, have you got the articles you wanted?" he asked. She just said 'yes' in a soft voice.

"Hello aunty." I greeted her. She just smiled a little. She is like that from the beginning. She speaks very little, but when she opens her matter, then she can demolish a person. Always well dressed, and thinking herself comparable to bollywood heroines is her special characteristic. Very shrewd and cunning. She is a *mithi churi.* She can cut you apart, before you realize anything.

"I think all the stuff I am going to say to you, would be better in meaning, if I could talk to your parents. But as you represent your family and they have full faith on you, we are talking to you." Uncle said, to which aunty just nodded in some sort of appreciation.

"So nice of you uncle. Ok. I am ready to take your blows." I said and chuckled. But astonishingly, he started to laugh. Aunty too joined him after few seconds. I got completely confused. Their laughter knew no bounds, as if I have just narrated some hilarious joke.

"Ohhh.... Sorry. Sorry Aditya, actually the way you said 'I am ready to take your blows' was incredible. Leave it. Lets come to the point." He said.

Her father's conditions ....

He started, "You truly know that, you are only my foolish and childish daughter's choice." I just remained still. He further said, "Actually, she has never seen any hardship in life. She was born with a silver spoon in her mouth. I do not know how she fell in love with you. The first day, you came to our house; I was very much annoyed to have the son of a mediocre family as my daughter's friend. It was she, who restricted my movements against you, and we are watching days like today.

I do not know how you can keep my daughter happy, if I get you two married. The living standard of your family is low too. But, I could not change anything. You are my silly girl's choice and I can not change it. I wonder how you can keep her happy in life with such level of..... Actually she does not know the difference between a dream and reality.

Every person, who gets lost in a desert, runs towards an oasis, but ends up finding only sands, never water. The person sees the mirage and realizes it to be the reality. Similarly, she is running after you, without knowing that it is an illusion."

The embankments of my patience broke down at these words. Before he could say anything further, I stood up and said in a high pitch,

"Excuse me uncle, if all these are the only things, you want to tell me, I am going. You are saying that my family as well as I have a base mentality. Let me tell you, yours is even lower. You can have plenty of money, but I must say, my family never does any business with me. For them the priority is my happiness. We never call a guest home and insult him with false allegations. And you compared me with an illusion, a mirage. Have you noticed that, you are indeed acting as the desert in which she has lost her away."

"Hey. Don't get so excited. Calm down. Please calm down. I am sorry for what I said. You know my nature. Every time, this happens to me. I want to say something and ultimately say something with a completely different meaning. Believe me, I never wanted to insult you. Please." He requested me to calm down. I then sat on the sofa and took some water from the bottle kept there.

"You perhaps know well that, we always had wanted to get her married to Arindam, my elder son's best friend. He is presently working as a CEO in a London based MNC. He owns his own flats in Delhi and London. He earns nearly twenty lakh rupees every month. So, evens you get hurt, I have to say that, you are nothing compared to him.

But the main thing is the so called 'love' for which she had chosen you over him as life partner. We decided to get her engaged to him and we ended up with this tragedy, disaster. That is the reason for which she tried to commit suicide.

I always wanted to get her married at the earliest possible, because I do not believe you two. Her mother thought that, the day you would turn 21, you two would certainly get married to each other. Then that would be completely unbearable for us. So we rushed her marriage and the result is in front of you." He was stopped by a text message I received.

I took out the phone and found it was from her.

"Please, excuse me. I will talk to you few minutes later." I said.

"Oh. Yes. Yes. Feel free. We have enough time. Finish you talk over phone, and then we would resume our talks." He replied instantly.

I opened my inbox and looked at the sms which said,

"*called ur home. Aunty told, u r in my home, gone to meet dad. Thanx. Luv u dear. Be cool n patient. Will be waiting 2 c u. luv u jaanu. I m missin my gublu sona badly. Mmmuuuaaaahhhh....*"

I at once replied her, "*ya. I m in ur home, with uncle n aunty. Interrogating me. Do nt know, where dey r heading. Ok. Bye. Luv u too dear. C u soon.*"

"Thanks uncle for your kind support. It was from Pooja. If I had not replied it by then, she would perhaps had sent a large number of messages. Those would be surely distracting." I said.

Hearing that their lovely daughter is still sending me messages from the hospital bed, the smile on his face disappeared. But in keeping with his rude and streaky nature, he resumed quickly and burst out again in a more ferocious way.

"I think you are well aware of her desire to become a professor. So we have decided that, after she gets her graduation degree, we would sent her either to Glasgow or Oxford for the masters as well as doctorate degree. Glasgow had always been her first choice. After all these incidents, we have finally realized that, It would be utter foolishness, to get her married against her will at this tender age. She must get an opportunity to establish her own identity in a dignified manner. She must be given a chance to fulfill the dreams she nurtures. What do you say?"

I was spellbound by these. I was mesmerized by her parent's thoughts. I said, "Why not uncle? She must pursue her studies further." I could make out the two sides of the same coin. One was this side that they were showing. And the other was that, they were are up to a plan called, 'out of mind, out of sight.' They thought that, if she remain in foreign for all those years, she would definitely forget me and my love. She would be so obsessed with the foreign country, that she would never think of coming back here for me. Then they would get the opportunity to get her married away, to whosoever they wanted.

"After her studies, I would not oppose your relationship with her. I myself would get her married to you. But in this regard, I want to say something. She is going to get very high level of education from a foreign university, and on the contrary, you are in an indigenous medical college. Further a doctor earns very less, nearly forty to fifty thousands a month, whatever degree he holds, before the age of 40. So in this regard, I want you to prove your eligibility as her groom. You must give us proof that, you can keep her happy in the future. You must assure us that, she would never be in any sort of distress.

"What!" I exclaimed. "What do you want to say? I have not understood the matter. Will you please tell me everything in a clear cut way?"

"Actually, I want you to fulfill some of my conditions. I can not give away my little princess to just anyone. My conditions are, firstly after you become a doctor, I want that you should owe a flat or house on your name. Secondly, you should have all the basic civic amenities of life, like tv, fridge, washing machine, and personal car.

And thirdly, you must have a monthly income of at least 40 thousand.

If you could fulfill these conditions, I will surely let her marry you. One more condition. Last, but not the least one, in all these years, when she would be in abroad, you would not try to communicate with her in any way and if she contacts you, you will not reciprocate.

I want you to prove your eligibility. Do it and she would be yours." He said in a perfectly grumpy voice.

"Ok I accept your proposal. But why shouldn't I contact her? It is completely unfair to set such a condition." I shouted.

"Don't shout. It will lead to nothing. It is my game, my rules and my prize. Do it or otherwise go away from her life." He said in a high pitch.

"What if, I do not accept all the stuff you are saying?" I asked.

"Nothing would happen as a whole. She would not be allowed to study any further and we will certainly get her married any how. By the way we are going to migrate to UK and settle. Now it is your decision, how you want her life to be shaped? Towards a certain career or an uncertain career." He replied.

"Sorry to say, what type of parents you are? Can't you see your daughter's happiness? you care only about family status!" I lost my cool.

"Not exactly, but yes I put the pride and glory of our prestigious family, above her happiness. If I could, I would never have allowed you to think, that you she can be yours." He said in a creepy manner, very much low pitched.

I thought for a moment. If I agree to these, he would never get her married. She would be able to pursue her studies and there would not be any problem. I believed in her, and whatever the conditions be she would not forget me. I had complete faith in her. So I agreed to the proposal.

"So sign on this court paper." Mr. Malhotra said.

I was shell shocked at this. I said, "No, I will not sign now. I would discuss it with her and then only I would sign."

"No you can not. You will never ever say even a single word, about all this to her. If you accept, sign it now or leave." He said and stood up.

"Good Bye." He said and went away. His wife followed him. I was left there completely alone.

In the real world, beside the dam ....

"So did you sign on the paper?" Pooja asked.

"What do you think, I am insane? I am not such a big fool, that I could not understand what he wanted. In the name of that signature, he would restrict all my movements. At least, we could talk to each other now. If I had signed, nothing would be left." I replied.

"Thanks. That is the reason why I love you so much. You always put love above everything." She said and at once hugged me. 'I love you' she said to me.

"I love you too darling." I told.

"Let's go to my room. I want something from you." She said.

I exclaimed, but I had no other option, than to abide by her order.

"Ouchh." She cried out.

"What happened?" I asked.

"I think, something hit my feet, stone chip most probably." No sooner than she said it, I sat down and in the mobile light examined her feet, but found nothing. She was constantly staring at me.

"Do you remember the day, when you kissed my feet?" she asked. I just smiled in return.

"It occurred just five or six months back. You came to our house, when I said that I was feeling some pain in the greater toe. You examined it and advised me to go to doctor. Your touch sends a current through my body. That day, you gently kissed my leg. Adi… thanks for all those lovely moments of my life. I have never realized that life is so beautiful. You gave the joy, the smile I desired. Thanks." She said.

"Same to you dear. Without you, I could not realize what love actually is. You are my life. I love you too. Ok. Leave these. Don't let me remember all the stuff again at this moment. I want to pass each and every moment today, with you, not with memories. Ok. Lets go." I said and we were returning. The fragrance of the orange flowers of the gulmohor tree, seemed to be very much soothing. The breeze filled each and every sense in my body. The whole environment seemed to be a perfect happy dream, like a utopia.

Inside her room .....

After spending nearly one and half hours outside, we entered her room making the least possible noise. I didn't want to get caught by her parents. So we remained almost silent, talking in whispers. Her room does not now look as I had last seen few months ago. All the furniture was missing except the bed and the dressing table. All the Shahrukh posters were missing too. The dim night bulb was still on. She offered me some water.

"So why had you called me here? Wats up sweetheart???" , I asked.

"I .... I .... I ....wanna .....", she mumbled.

"Wats it yaar ? Speak it out? *Baanda hajir hai sarkar , ap jo bhi chahenge , wohi hoga....to kya kehna chahti hain aap....meri jaanejigar?"*, I said.

"Stop irritating me. Sona I am serious. I want something from you. I want to have you at the fullest. I want to be yours forever.", she said. I got confused as well as nervous, because ... I can't express myself. "Can't you say anything clearly? What do you want dear?" , I tried to look normal , but she sensed my nervousness. According to her, I am a good actor who can hide emotions very easily, but when with her I am a complete blunder.

"I wanna have that with you"......

"Wanna do what ?" , I could sense her intentions but as usual I was confused as to what to do next. Like all the other situations she took the initiative.

"I want to have sex with you." , she said and came near me. She put her head on my chest. Tears rolled down her cheeks. I was perplexed. Completely confused. I have always wanted to have sex with her. But whenever I approached it she always changed the topic. In all these years I had gone completely extrovert even in front of her. But when she is asking for sex, I was.... Completely out of my mind. Firstly I was unable to believe what I was hearing.

"Whaaa... what do you said? You want to sex!!!! Please, I am not in any mood of amusement. I am not happy any more. Don't make always such filthy pranks." I replied. Astonishingly, she did not smile.

"Ya sona. I am 100 percent serious. I want to have sex with you. I want to have you at the fullest. I always wanted to live my life with you, wanted to make a family. But everything is futile, everything is gone. So, I don't want to let these moments go by. I want to live my life in these moments. Please. I ... you are perhaps thinking that, I have gone completely mad. But I am not. I only want to be yours. Only by this I will become yours, and will remain yours for the rest of my life." She said.

Tears were still streaming down her cheeks, she had the most beautiful eyes of the world I had ever noticed. There was no denying the fact that; I too got into the situation. I accepted her proposal. But I was hesitant to do as I didn't have a condom. I told her about the condition. To which she laughed and said, "I believe you dear. Its my safe period. You need not to worry. Even if it happens, you would not be held responsible. I am older than you. So, don't hesitate. Come. Lets have an earthly enjoyment of love."

The next moment we were passionately kissing each other. Actually

I too had wanted to have sex with her, nagged her for it, but she had always turned me down. But today, even when I was with the most beautiful girl of the world, I am still not happy. Actually the grief of losing her a few hours later was still haunting me.

I don't know how girls can understand everyone so easily..... I told her not to cry, though I was myself crying. After several minutes of kissing, she started to take off my clothes. She put me on her bed. She sat over me. I put my hands on her breasts. I was on the seventh heaven. Now I was too enjoying the sudden excitement and turn in the life.

"*Upar se hi karoge kya?* Be a man and take off my clothes sweetheart. You are such a dumbo. Even in all these years I have not been able to make a complete man out of you... "she said and opened her top. I was mesmerized by her such forwardness. I myself think sometimes that, she had all the characters of a boy. But this was not the time to think anymore, it's the time to follow the instincts.

We then again engaged in deep smooch. My hands were wandering all over her breasts. After a few minutes we had shed all our clothes. In front of me, there was standing the most beautiful girl of the universe absolutely nude. I pounced on her belly region and licked throughout. She moaned slowly. I got the sign. She was turning on. I encircled my tongue around her navel and moved it in a soft manner. With one hand I was exploring her breasts and the other was on her lowers, exploring her soft groin. The aroma of the vagina was intoxicating. It was absolutely mesmerizing. I was in a stage of utopia. There was no loss, no gain, no pain, only the wildest sensation of the nature.

The next moment she turned up and in a semi standing position, we again kissed each other passionately. She was completely overwhelmed by my masculinity. She took it in her hand and kissed the top. I was just feeling weightlessness. She sucked me off. I jerked and throbbed my cock out of her mouth to unload on her breasts. She lay down on the couch and I came over her. I then started the foreplay again. She was in ecstasy. She signaled me to enter her. After nearly five or six attempts I succeeded. My each and every stroke left her gasping at the beautiful as well as lustful time. The moment was telling upon us and in five minutes we both came at the same instant.

We just did it. Not so passionately, but in a harsh manner. It was a first time sex and most probably our last with each other. Tears came to our eyes. Both of us were breathing heavily. Finally we parted. It was 5:30 am then. We washed ourselves and got dressed. I kissed her forehead and her lower lip. She moaned and started crying.

"Why do you love me so much? Why do you do whatever I ask you for? Why are you so good? Why do you love me?" she broke into sobs.

"Love... I can only say a few line from the song of *Westlife.*

It does not take much to learn,

When the bridges that you burn, leave you stranded feeling alone.

It does not take much to cry, when you are living in a lie.

And deceiving that someone who cares

If I could turn back the time, I would put you first in my life.

And I would risk it all for you, to prove my love is true....". I said and gave a soft smile.

"Please take me with you. Let's go away somewhere; no one would be able to find us. I will die without you. Please don't go.", she was sobbing. I deliberately took her in my arms and hugged her.

"Don't fear. I will return. I will certainly bring you back. I promise you to fulfill all your parent's wishes. I promise dear. Believe in me. I will never forget you. I can't forget my life.

I will stand by you forever... you can take my breath away ...

You are the drug that keeps me from dying.... May be I'm addicted...

But I'm trying... I'm trying... I'm trying...", I said.

"I will be waiting for you till the time you don't come. I will wait for you till the ultimatum. You will be in my thoughts all the time. You will be in my every tear; you will be in my smile. You will certainly be with me every time. Even at the cost of my life, I will prove that, I had only loved you and could be only yours. Frankly speaking, I do not think Dad would let me take admission in any college. He will try to get me married as soon as possible. Here he is bound, due to your presence, as there are many relatives. He just can not avoid them so easily. He would certainly try his best in a foreign country, where there would be no one to stop him. The law there is very rigid, more pronounced than that in our country. But they will not leave any stone unturned to keep me out of your reach. But I must say that, I will oppose them every moment. I know all will ultimately go in vain, but I will try. At least, it will give me some sort of internal satisfaction. They will torture me both physically and mentally. But I will never let them tread over my heart and feelings, so easily. When the embankments of my patience would get devastated, I will end my life. It would teach them some sort of lesson about love. Hope they might realize their fault ultimately. I will kill myself, when I would realize that, maximum damage has been done. Now I am saying, let's go away from everything." She said in choked voice.

"Don't talk about ending you life again. Only fools and cowards do not fight and succumb to death. Why do you think that, if you die, all problems would be solved? You are with me and I am always yours, though you fear about the future. Don't be dear. We are with each other, that is the main thing. Whatever the conditions are, you are not going to disbelieve the other. Only this could save us dear. Please do not fear. And if you do not want to go there, leave them. Come with me. Everything will be fine again." I said in a rough voice to show off that, I was still alright. But within I was bleeding at every inch of the heart.

"It's not so easy. If I go with you, what would you do to earn your livelihood? You would take money from your dad. But to me it would be weird. A few moments earlier, I wanted to flee with you. But there would be many problems. Police will not leave you under their orders. They would watch every corner of the world to find us. Various charges would be laid down on you. Your career would be gone. That's the thing they want to do. They want to destroy you. But I don't want you to be lost due to me. You have responsibilities to your family. If something happens to you, where would they stand? So…… I give you two options. First, leave me and the second one, you have to wait, not expecting that, your wait would give you flowers. I must say, leaving me is the better option. You are a good person. Why are you wasting your life on me? You have a very bright future. You must not indulge yourself with me. You will experience only pain and sorrow with me. Forget me dear." She said in a crackled voice.

"What the hell are you talking about? You are asking me to forget you and move with the flow of life. Have you forgotten that, it's you who tried to end life for not once, but twice? How can I ever forget you? How? Can I forget to take my breath? No naaa….. Then how can I forget you?" I said.

The next moment, we were in a tight hug. Tears were rolling down.

Many thoughts were coming to my mind. There was a complete blackout in my mind. I was at the verge of losing all of happiness and hope. I was unable to do anything. I wanted from the core of heart to let the time stop. But nothing happened. Time was passing. Finally the watch struck 6.00. I realized that the time to leave had come. There was nothing left. I said only one thing to her before I departed.

"When I am with you, eternity is a step away
My love continues to grow with each passing day.
If I had a single flower for every time I think about you,
Then I would walk forever in my garden of love.
I had written your name in my heart,
And it will stay there forever, whatever time it would be.
Forever and always, I will love you……."

"I love you too." She said and kissed my forehead. I reciprocated the same to my nearest and dearest one.

I came out. She was still standing by the side of the window. The sun was about to rise in a melancholy mood. I wanted to hold time back but I couldn't. Once again I was defeated by the hands of destiny.

I went straight to the hill top and throw out all the agony inside me. I shouted at the highest pitch of my voice. I asked the Almighty ….. "Why you always do this to me???" I shouted again and again. But no answer came from anywhere. I was crying, actually shedding the anguish inside me.

After nearly half an hour I came downstairs and proceeded towards my home. I remembered the face of my mom, who might, had not slept throughout the night. I passed through all the deserted roads, which were now getting the crowd of the morning walkers to the horticulture park.

But among all the crowd of children with their grand parents and young couples, I was completely alone. There were no colors; there was only darkness all over. Every community seemed to be a gloomy community. It was like the attack of dementors, seemed that all happiness from the world is perhaps lost. There was nothing, nothing, nothing. Everything was lost. The fire of love seemed to be burnt out. Time suddenly slowed down by some magical spell all around. I was lost in the moments of the recent past. They were haunting me. But somehow I reached home after all the hectic night. I was left alone with my thoughts, completely lost in the pitch black darkness inside my soul.

I returned home ....

I returned home nearly at 6.45 am. I was tired as well as devastated in all senses. I was not able to bear anything more.

As I entered my home, Mom came to me hastily and asked a number of questions, "Are you alright? Is everything fine? You know, I waited for you the whole night. You said, you will meet her and return at the earliest possible. But you returned after the whole night. Where have you been?"

"I was in her home, better say in her room." I replied.

"What? It is very bad to tell lies to your mother. Tell the truth, where have you been last night." She asked.

"Adi's 'Believe it or not', it is indeed true by verbatim. I went to her and then she came out of her home. Spent a lot of time under the sky, and then we were together in her room. Thanks to my goodness, no one noticed us. And everything was absolutely fine. We both treasured memories comparable to a life time. We collected memories that are valuable more than a treasure. We just..... We......" I could not speak any more.

I just cried. I was totally shattered. I was unable to control myself. The whole night was filled with a number of mental ups and downs. The pressure was taking its toll. My heart sank in the memories. I could not cry in front of her and expel my emotions outside. I just drank the glasses of poison last night with an apparently smiling face. But near Mom all bondages came to an end and I could not restrict myself.

"Hey kid..... Don't cry dear. I know your mental status. Please stop crying. The pain is inevitable, but you have to suffer it and tolerate it. You can not escape that kid. It is your fate; you have to undergo the pain. Destiny is the greatest thing son, the more you try to fight it, the more it treats you badly. You have to identify the way, your luck takes you to. You can run, you can hide, but you can not escape those, which is written in your fate. You have to accept it." Mom said.

I somehow restrained myself. I stopped crying. She just hugged me and kissed my forehead. It was so relieving that, I could not explain. It was the most soothing experience in the last few hours.

"Do you want to say anything more?" Mom asked.

"Mom she is going. She is going. There is no way back. I can not live without her. I am unable to bear this. I can not take her departure. I am lost." Tears again rolled down.

"You are my brave son na??? Why are you crying? If you lose all hopes, how will she survive? Stop crying. Believe in God, my heart says everything will be fine dear. And I just warn you, if Arun, finds you crying, you know yourself the kind of pranks he would play with you." Mom said and I smiled I bit.

"Mom I want to sleep. Please don't let bro disturb me. And most importantly, wake me up by 8.30. Her train is at 11. I had promised to reach her home by 9.30. She wants me to arrive at such fag end, to avoid any unwanted situation." I said.

"Ok. Go and get some sleep son. You had a hard time last night."

At her home at morning ....

I went to her home again on the same day, for the second time at exactly the time she had asked to. I found two Mercedes standing outside. I recognized the blue one, which belong to the Malhotra family, but could not make out whom the other one belonged to.

As I entered her house, I found that there were two other families, who had perhaps come to bid them a farewell. But my sight was looking for the most beautiful girl of the world. I passed the families. They looked at me as a stranger. They were looking hard at me. But my swift movements amazed them more. I found her outside the drawing room. Finding me, she instantly came to me and we hugged casually. She was dressed in a maroon salwar kameez with golden print. On the other side there was a very handsome and well dressed guy. I identified him at once as Arindam the rich boy her parents wanted her to marry'.

Looking at us, Mr. Malhotra came forward.

"Hello Aditya. How are you? When did you come from Kolkata? Pooja why don't you go and meet the Kapoor family? Your brother is also there." he said, with some sort of frustration after finding me there. She left the spot, still looking at me. Her eyes had conveyed something, which only I could understand.

"Hello uncle. I am fine. I came last night. Just wanted to see off her. That's it." I replied.

"Sure. Sure. So nice of you that you came here today. None of her friends had come to meet her. You are her only true friend." He said in a low voice.

I, in a rather lower voice said him, "How could not I come? I have promised to be with her for her whole life." only he was able to hear it.

"I do not want any scene to be created here. Please leave this place." He said in utter disgust.

"What? You are taking away her from me for such a long time, and I can not even see her properly for the last time. How could you think that? I do not want anything wrong, to happen now, when she is leaving. I too want her to give off a happy send off.

As I do not believe and respect you any more, I request you not to get in my way. I will keep a distance from her. But, sorry to say, if you keep bumping into me, it would not be good for you." I warned him.

"What are you doing here dad, Mr. and Mrs. Kapoor are waiting for you. Oh... Aditya. How did you come here? Everything fine na?" her elder brother asked. He came with that aristocrat chap. It left no confusion in my mind that, this is Mr. Arindam.

"Oh. Let me have the privilege to introduce you to him." Said her brother.

"Aditya, he is Arindam Chawdhury, my best friend and CEO in a MNC in UK. And Arin this is Aditya, Pooja's best friend, now a medical student, MBBS." He introduced us.

We shook hands cordially. And at that moment she arrived.

"Adi, firstly sorry as I had to go leaving you behind. Oh. You two perhaps had met each other. Hey, what is in your hand?" she talked, never looking at the lad standing beside. This was the first time we were seeing each other. I had heard his name many a times from her mouth. Perhaps he was too aware of me as the lover of his girl.

"Wait. Wait. I thought of giving it to you when we are by ourselves. You always rush every matter." I said, while Mr. Arindam , stood still looking at us. I held her arms and dragged her to some corner. I looked at him. He was still there looking at us, pretending of watching some other object.

I opened the small, red colored velvet box. There was a small gold pendent with a dazzling beauty. Her eyes sparkled when she saw it.

She said in a low voice, "So nice of you dear. Thanks. You bought it for me. Thanks, it is the best gift I ever had."

"Actually, I had not brought it. It belongs to Mom. Dad brought it. It was his first gift to her, after marriage. She had always desired, to have you as her daughter in law. She has worn it only once. To her, it is a lucky charm and so she always keeps it in her bag. She now wants you to keep it. She believes that, a hard time is coming in your life. You would most probably lose all hopes. During those days, this pendant will keep the flame of hope alive. She wanted to give it to you personally, but it is impossible. So, she handed it to me. So keep it."

"I know you do not believe in things like, 'lucky charm'. But I must say, the dark days are coming. The only thing we can do is to keep faith in each other and love each other, whatever the distance between us is. Keep it as the token of my mom's love for you. Keep it as my remembrance. I do not know, whether it would show any magic or not, it would certainly keep your memory blazing with the thought that, there is someone here, who would be waiting for you forever." I said.

"Pooja.... Pooja.... Where are you? The guests are gone. We have to hurry dear. It's been five past ten. Where are.... Oh you are here with Aditya. Hope I am not disturbing you." Her mother came shouting.

"Nothing at all Aunty. We are not disturbed. I have finished. Ok. Pooja I better go away, I can not...." Before I could finish, she snatched my words and said, "What the hell 'go away' is? You are not going anywhere. You will go with us to the station. We couldn't pass our life hand in hand; will you not even accompany me to the station?" her voice mumbled and eyes got damp, so were mine. Her mother was gone by then.

"Of course. With you I am ready even to go to hell. Surely I will go with you. But please keep a distance from me. Your family will never miss any opportunity to trash you." She nodded.

I was about to go out, when she stopped me. "Wouldn't you help me in putting it?" She said and handed over the pendant and necklace to me. She turned backwards and lifted her hair; I put the necklace in her neck. She was looking amazingly beautiful.

I then went out and get into my car, an Alto. It was the second car we have. I, Mom and bro ride it. Dad never rides it. When all of us go out together we use Dad's car, Maruti.

In the station on that deserted day ....

We reached the station at 10.30. The train was to come at platform number 1. On the next platform, there were many college goers, waiting for their, local train to Asansol. Most of the students, who studied in different colleges of Asansol, take that local train.

All of them were waiting at the platform. But I decided to keep some distance, and stood nearly a hundred meters away from the family, under the foot over bridge.

She noticed me watching her and came up to me. I could clearly sense the pain she had been feeling then. I too was in the same distressed mood and I must say, I was about to cry. Somehow we managed to control. But when she grabbed my hands, she could not control herself any more. She put her head on my chest and started crying. I put my hands on her head and tried to console her. I saw many faces turning towards us. Some college goers whistled. But I was in no mood to think about them.

Suddenly I noticed her mother signaling something to Arindam, and he started to walk towards us. "Hey, stand straight. Many people are looking at us." I said to her.

"Let them see. You are afraid, inspite of being a boy. You always turn me down." She said.

"For your kind information mam, your much desired Arindam is approaching us." She hastily looked up.

"Hi Aditya.... You two seems to be very good friends," He said in a satanic voice. "You would perhaps miss her very much after her departure. But we have to go with time. Time makes you forget everything. After all she is going to make a very good career. Don't be upset dude. Oh. Pooja, Aunty is calling you." She rushed to her Mom.

"So why are you all going Delhi?" I asked.

"Hadn't you asked her about this?" he questioned.

"Truly speaking, no. I had not asked that. On the phone, we talked only about ourselves. We discussed nothing more." I replied.

"Well uncle owes some property in Gurgaon and Allahabad. We would first sell them off and then would go to UK." He answered.

"How long is it going to take?" I asked and he just waved his head to answer in negative.

"You are a doctor naa?" he asked.

I chuckled a little and replied, "I am just a medical student, not doctor." After that he said that, he too had the desire to become doctor.

"Arindam... Come here." Her father shouted.

"Yes, I am coming. So, if you get the opportunity someday, come and visit us. I do not think any one of them would return to India again. Lastly, Sorry Aditya, I am taking away your most precious thing with myself. Don't get hurt dude. Ok. Bye." He went away.

I looked at them. Her mother and brother were saying something to her and she was nearly weeping. I thought of going to her, but I did not. I was sure that, they must be having a quarrel over her behavior towards me. Inside myself, I realized that, if I went to her, it would act like gun powder pouring on flames.

Yatrigan kripiya dhyan de, nayi delhi jaanewali poorva express, kuchi der main platform sankhya ek par aa rahi hai. Dhanyabad."

I turned my gaze from them and looked at the groups of college goers. By then their numbers had gone up. Suddenly I heard a shout from her against her parents. Next moment she, rushed towards me. And before I could understand anything, she nearly dragged me by force and kissed me directly on my lips. I was mesmerized. Many college goers shouted and whistled at us. There was a lot of clapping.

Then the train arrived and she went away. Just waved and said good bye. They boarded the train and it started. She stood at the entrance and extended her hand and face outside. I quickly ran and held her hands. I could barely say, 'I love you' and the train gathered speed. I kept standing at the end of the platform, completely broken. I was crying. I knelt down, looked up and said to God, "Why did you do this to me?"

Finally I came out of the deserted station. Mom and Dad were standing there. I ran to Mom and hugged her. I burst into tears.

The last letter ....

After she left, I shut myself in my room. I returned to college, but spoke very little. All my days and nights passed remembering her. One day after a month, I got an e mail alert on my mobile. I opened the browser to get internet access. I was astonished after finding that, it was her mail.

Hi Sona,

I reached here safely. It is most probably the Greater Kailash area. Mom and Dad had put me in some sort of interim prison. I am writing you this mail from bhaiyaa's laptop without his permission. After the time I had, entered the apartment, I was not allowed to go out of the door even once. The trio thrashed me over the railway station incident. Arindam also joined the party. I can not believe them any more. They created so much fuss in the train, that the other co passengers intervened and rescued me. I told you na, they are planning something.

I do not know, whether these are my last words or not. But in this letter, I want to ask you for something. Promise me, whatever I would ask for, you would give it to me.

You have clearly understood in all this time that, we can never be together again, whatever we do. I do not know about you, but I have realized that, we are not sharing our future with each other.

My future is completely darkened. You are my only hope in this pitch black darkness. Promise me, one day you will become a very good doctor. Forget me. I am the darkest chapter of your life. I have nothing, but only pain to give to you. Please leave me. Start your life from a new point. I humbly request you to, move forward in life and fulfill your parent's dreams.

Finally, do not think about me. I mean, never waste your time thinking about me. I can clearly see my future. I do not know the limit, to which I can bear all the sufferings. The moment I would realize that, there is no way back, I will definitely end up my life. My life and death takes your name. You are always in my every breath. I will prove to all of them, that I had loved only one person, that is you. I can never belong to anyone else. I will prove this by my life. I can only be yours. None can take me away from you.

Always keep smiling and live the life at the fullest I know whatever I am saying would seem to be just advices, but these are requests. You will be in my heart for ever. You will always be in my thoughts. I will see the world with your eyes; I will always smile with you.

I love you and will always keep you loving till my last breath. Give my best wishes to Uncle, Aunty and Arun. Love you sona. I will never forget my sweet lolly pop. I love you jaanu.

Good bye........... Tata..... I will miss you very much sona....

Only yours,

Pooja Malhotra ...